To Handcuff Lightning

Grapevine Card Company
P.O. Box 1134
Woodstock, GA 30188-1134
USA

Copyright © 2007 by Sharon KD Hoskins
All rights reserved, including the right of reproduction in whole or in part in any form.

For discount, bulk purchases, contact Grapevine Cards at 1-866-501-7800 or by email at
books@grapevinecards.com

Designed by Sharon KD Hoskins

Cover graphic objects:
Copyright © 2004 Herma Photo Collection

Manufactured in the United States of America

ISBN: 978-0-9794576-0-9

To Handcuff Lightning

Sharon KD Hoskins

Grapevine Card Company
Woodstock, Georgia 30188
USA

For Alberta, Viola, and Effie Naomi
*Because you know where all
the bodies are buried.*

To handcuff lightning, put a hold on thunder,
Run through the graveyard, and
Put the dead to wonder.

Will Lee Clover, 1921-1992

To Handcuff Lightning

THE PLACE

"When I get some age on me, I'm gonna have me a beer."
—Screamie, age 3

"That's the first thing that little girl said to me," says Algie (al-GEE'), laughingly shaking her head from side-to-side. She sets a plate of hot food in front of a customer sitting next to Benny Thomas, the bar owner from across the street. "Before that Benny," she continues. "It was a whole lot of screaming or no sound at all!"

It's October 1957 in Dayton, Ohio. Algie "owns" The Place, a small restaurant on Dayton's Westside at the corner of Germantown and Hawthorn Streets. The Great Miami River is the dividing line between black Dayton and white Dayton. Nearly everybody on the Westside is black; everybody on the Eastside is white.

Screamie is the daughter of Early Bird, Algie's man-friend. The child earned her nickname for her incessant and unwarranted screaming, not because her real name, Máxke[1] (mah-SKI'), is so hard for most people to pronounce. The child's maternal grandmother is an American Indian and she gave her granddaughter that descriptive name. Screamie is yellow-red. She has fine, sandy brown

---

[1] Máxke is a Delaware Indian (Ohio tribe) word that means red.

hair that is not thick enough to hide her scalp nor long enough to gather together into pigtails. Instead, it grows like a veil of gauze sprouting softly atop her tiny head. She has large, chocolate pupils that nearly fill-up her eyeballs. Her translucent, pink lips are so thin, that from a distance, they look like one lip instead of two.

When Algie first met Early's little girl, she let go a loud, dry wail that was bigger than the size of the child. Algie's reply was to reach down and place a small piece of cornbread into her open mouth. "She can't holler if her mouth is full of food," Algie told Early. Nowadays, the little girl rarely screams, at least not at The Place. Algie reassures Screamie that the unfamiliar faces peering over the counter are friends who just stopped by to eat.

Screamie occasionally blurts out comments that are a mix of the isolated words she hears from the conversations overhead. Most times, she strings the words together into senseless phrases. But to the amusement of Algie and others, her words sometimes come together into understandable statements with a comical twist.

Neither too thin nor too can fat, Algie easily lift three-year-old Screamie into her arms. The child never complains and doesn't make a sound as long as she's cradled in Algie's arms. During the week, Screamie lives with her mother and three other siblings; each with different fathers. But on weekends she eats, sleeps, and plays with a doll that is more raggedy than Ann on her mat behind the counter right, next to Algie's stool.

Two of Algie's grown daughters are quite fond of the little red baby, however, a third daughter has not interest in her at all. But it's Algie that takes the most care, stroking Screamie's hair and changing her clothes, whether they need it or not. Algie's affection for the child has little to do with her relationship with Early. It's the "redness" of the baby that has bound her to Máxke.

"Early around?" Benny asks. "I hope not," he whispers to himself.

"Yes," Algie replies. "He's next door at Crook's."

Benny looks directly at Algie, and before he loses his nerve, goes ahead with the question he's wanted to ask her. "How does that child's mother feel about you keeping her all the time?"

Algie sets a bowl of peach cobbler in front of the customer next to Benny, and walks back into the kitchen for the next order without a word.

"Oh, crap," he mutters to himself. "That's too much, too soon, Benny. You've blown it now."

Algie soon returns from the kitchen with a paper plate full of hot food wrapped in aluminum foil and hands it to the waiting customer at the open end of the lunch counter. She then grabs the coffee pot from the burner and freshens Benny's coffee. Without looking up at him, she finally says, "You know, she came in here once Benny. Just stood there and stared at me from across the counter. Then turned around and walked right back out without saying a word."

Relieved that she has finally responded to him, Benny quickly follows with, "What did you do then?"

"I told Early about it and he confronted her." Algie continues. "She told him she just wanted to see what I looked like. She heard I had three grown daughters, so at least I know how to deal with girls. It don't bother her that Screamie is here because she's got three other kids at home. Any day without just child of is a blessing. "

"How do you feel about it though Algie?" asks Benny. "After all, she's right. Your girls are all grown."

"Screamie's no bother," says Algie, almost defensively. "And, since none of my girls has brought forth a life yet, I enjoy having the baby girl around."

Benny watches the heat rising from his coffee for a minute and takes a sip. "A little at a time, little at a time," he reassures himself. Shifting gears, he switches the conversation to a less sensitive subject.

"How long now has this spot been a restaurant? Is it two or three years?"

"It's been three years, Benny." Algie calls back to him from the kitchen. "And prayer and hard work is what got it done. Besides, a restaurant is a much better place for me and my girls than a pawn shop, especially with their Daddy gone now."

Benny nods sympathetically in agreement.

In 1949, Edward "Eddie Mack" Clover and Algie Julia Jordan-Clover arrived in Dayton, Ohio from Dublin, Georgia with their family; three daughters and Algie's mother, Chauncey. Their daughters are Tressie (now 26), Viola (now 24), and Honey (now 22).

Prior to their leaving, several Clover family members had already made the trip north. Despite the exodus North, Algie was not convinced the move was the right thing for her family. She expressed her concern to Edward (she never called him Eddie Mack) every single day of the weeks and months leading up to their departure. That day finally came. Without complaint, Algie helped load up their belongings into the used 1941 Buick sedan purchased specifically for this trip. She didn't voice her disappointment during the 11-hour car ride to Dayton, nor at anytime since their arrival. She didn't see the point. They were here now and she could make the best of any situation.

Eddie Mack's cousin, Willie "Crook" Clover, had found a house for them to rent in Dayton, so they stopped there instead of going on to Detroit. Eddie Mack quickly found work at Dessi Airplane Parts. She needed to work to help out, so Algie took a job at the pawn shop which was only a 10-minute walk from the house. Six months after she began working there as a clerk, the "owner" of the pawn shop decided to move back home to St. Louis. Algie and Eddie Mack saw an opportunity. They would transform the pawn shop into a restaurant. Eddie Mack didn't like the clientele his wife dealt with at the pawn shop. And, a restaurant was something they could work at together.

Four days after they made their first rent payment on the restaurant they named The Place, Eddie Mack dropped dead at Dessi from an aneurysm. Overwhelmed by grief, shock, and the reality of suddenly becoming a widow, Algie immediately began making plans to return home to Georgia. That was exactly what her mother, Chauncey, urged her to do. However, her three daughters had other plans. Back in Georgia, they had pleaded with their parents to move north and give them a chance for a life doing anything but slave-farming. They were not going back! Besides, most of the family was gone now anyway.

Algie did want a better life for her girls and it was true, there wasn't much for them back home. So, she decided the Bible would make the decision for the family; not her fears and not their youthful determination. Three days after she laid her husband of 30 years to rest in Greencastle Cemetery (she couldn't afford to take him back home for burial), Algie laid her right hand on her grandmother Julia's bible and prayed for God to show her the way. Like her grandmother had taught her, she slept with the bible underneath her pillow. As soon as she opened her eyes the next day, she rolled over, opened up the bible, and this scripture greeted her eyes:

"Let [YOUR] manner of life be free of the love of money, while YOU are content with the present things. For he has said: "I will by no means leave you nor by any means forsake you." So that we may be of good courage and say: "Jehovah is my helper; I will not be afraid. What can man do to me?"[2]

Algie closed the bible and decided to stay.

With the loss of her husband's income, however, she had to start out by serving lunches right next to the moldy, fake fur coats; tarnished "gold" watches; and other assorted pawned goods. Algie prepared the food at home and used a hot plate to keep it warm at work. Three long years later, the

---

[2] Hebrews 13:5-6. New World Translation of the Holy Scriptures, published by Watchtower Bible and Tract Society of New York, Inc.

transformation was complete. In the beginning, all of her daughters helped out at The Place, but only Tressie, the eldest, now works there full-time.

Benny never ate any meals at the pawn shop while it was undergoing its' transformation, but he stopped by often to chat with Algie even when her husband was still alive. He now crosses the street every day, except Sunday (the bar is closed), to eat lunch and dinner at her restaurant. Benny can't figure out why Algie hasn't gotten the hint. He's much better for her than that day worker who doesn't know where his next dollar is coming from, and even has the nerve to dump his daughter off on her every weekend. Benny was shocked to learn Algie had taken up with Early. He thought his reserved, slow style would appeal to the widow. He had no idea some young sport was moving in on his territory. Maybe she's mad because he never bought anything from her while she was struggling to make a restaurant. But Benny hasn't given up yet. Early's good thing will run out sooner or later, and he'll be right here waiting to step in.

Algie looks younger than her 48 years, and Early looks older than his 33. Therefore, few people suspect there is any age difference between them at all.

At 4'11" and 110 pounds, Algie is small for an adult woman and she has to sit on a stool behind the counter in order to see and to reach across it. She

wears no make-up on her heart-shaped face —
never has. Her skin is an even shade of ocean sand
brown with no undertones or age spots. Only the
tiniest lines have started to emerge across her
forehead and around the corners of her mouth.
The dark, liquid pupils of Algie's eyes are stark
still. She always seems to be looking straight
ahead, even during intimate conversations. Her
doll's eye stare makes some people uncomfortable,
but others, like Benny, are hypnotized by it.

Algie styles her lightly salted hair into a thick,
coiled, ponytail held together by a single rubber
band. Wispy, wayward strands float out of the
band creating a wild halo around her head.
Despite the abundance of hair on her head, her
eyebrows are almost nonexistent. They are thin,
short arches that fade over her heavily lashed
eyelids into nothingness. Algie's nostrils are like
two small dots placed on the center of her face.
Even her ears are small; perfectly shaped and
aligned on either side of her head.

But none of these features are what come to mind
when people think of the little woman who runs
The Place. Rather, it's her puckered lips which
appear permanently poised for a kiss. When Algie
was a child, kids teased her about those lips calling
her Ducky. As an adult, many would be suitors
have tried to steal a kiss from them. Nowadays,
she moistens her lips each morning with a little
petroleum jelly, no lipstick. Algie does this to

counter their propensity for dryness which makes her subconsciously lick her lips, drawing even more unwanted attention to them.

Everyday, she wears a knee-length, short-sleeve dress that has a tailored collar and buttons up the front. She sews the garments herself using either floral or paisley prints. Over the dress, she layers a an unbuttoned, white duster that stops just short of her knees; aligned with the hemline of the dress. The pockets of the duster are deep enough for her wallet and keys so she doesn't have to carry a purse. She completes the outfit with a pair of white nurse's shoes and seamless, flesh toned stockings. She has been mistaken for a nurse while standing in line at the bank, but wears the duster and shoes because it is the most comfortable outfit she's found for working in all day. The only change to her attire is the addition of a heavy wool coat, over the ensemble, in the winter.

While not unfriendly, Algie is not a talker. She answers when spoken to and speaks only when she has something to say.

Algie's daughters have not questioned their mother about her relationship with Early. The only time the two are together is at The Place. Early has never been invited to the house and their mother has never left home or the restaurant to go anywhere with him. Besides, he will never replace their father and they feel certain their plain, unromantic mother won't marry again.

Algie was not initially attracted to Early, a younger man with no money and no ambition. Tall and straight, Early's body is a long, lean column of black, shiny copper. His short, straight teeth look as if they have been purposely filed down to perfect white squares. Early's eyes have such a slant that many friends jokingly call him the "black China-man". He's starting to go a little bald on top, but says he's "not bothered by that all".

Early is a day laborer who first came into The Place because he was cold standing on the corner outside waiting for a job. If he gets picked up for a job he might be gone for days. More often, he is back in a couple of hours.

Early liked the little lady who ran the restaurant because she was friendly and didn't ask too many questions. Soon he began making it a habit to stop in for coffee, even when it wasn't cold outside. If Early didn't get a job, he'd come inside and sit at the counter, drinking coffee and talking.

In a short while, he had told Algie about his military time in Korea. The reason his mother named him Early (he was born a week early at 3:00 AM), and all about his daughter, Máxke, and why he nicknamed her Screamie. Early talked about his family in Texas and why he came to Ohio after he had gotten out of service, instead of going back home.

In time, he asked Algie if his mail could come to The Place because his government checks for his military service supposedly never arrived at the rooming house where he lives on South Euclid Avenue. He then begin showing up on weekends with his daughter in-tow.

They've never been out on a date, but everyone knows Algie and Early are a couple.

Early eats all his meals, for free, at The Place and turns over most of his daily wages to Algie. "Just keeps a little walking around money in my pocket," he explains, whenever she asks if he needs more money. Algie opens every piece of mail he receives and even signs and cashes his government checks for him. She gives him his rent money and he lets her know of any additional expenses he might have, such as money requests from Screamie's mother.

Periodically, Early's mother in Texas will send him a letter and Algie reads it to him. His mother's writing is more scrawl than actual script, but not much different from Algie's own mother's patient, slow attempts to write. Chauncey had insisted that her only child learn to read and write and complete what ever schooling was available to her. Early, on the other hand, quit school in the 6th grade and admits, "I couldn't read or write that good when I was in school!"

After reading the letter from Texas, Algie then asks Early how he would like to answer his mother. She jots down a short note, summarizing his response, and folds a couple of dollars into the envelope before she mails it.

Early is nothing like her Edward.

Edward, who was Eddie Mack to everyone except Algie, had a medium frame with broad shoulders and muscular arms shaped and sculpted by years of hard farm labor that began when he was only 10 years old. His ice cream vanilla skin was dotted with tiny red freckles from head-to-toe, and his sunset red hair was locked into tight curls, each with its own unique cowlick. Eddie Mack's mother was white and he had her green-hazel eyes — or so he'd been told. She left him with his father's mother the day he was born and headed to California. His father, Charlie Clover, came-and-went and was dead (murdered) before his infant son began walking.

Eddie Mack was known around Dublin as a dependable, able-bodied man who took care of his family and didn't owe anybody a thing — not even a favor. Both women and men were drawn to his wide, genuine smile that was never missing from his face.

When Eddie Mack first came to call on Algie, Chauncey tore into him with a relentless verbal attack. "No, he could not come to call at the house." "No, he could not take her daughter on a picnic." "No, he could not walk her daughter home from church."

Through it all, Eddie Mack just smiled — not at Chauncey — but directly at Algie.

Three months after he first saw her, sitting next to her grandmother in church, Eddie Mack rolled his truck (engine off) into Algie's front yard. She saw him through the window and ran to open the front door. She stood in the doorway and silently watched him approach her. Eddie Mack walked up, gently took Algie's hand, and led her to his truck. They quickly drove away, leaving the front door standing wide open and a bewildered and furious Chauncey yelling after them.

They were married that same day; she was 17, he was 21.

Algie is Chauncey's one and only living baby. Back in Dublin, most families — black or white — had six or more children. The three sisters before Algie all died before they were a year old. And, there's a dead brother (2-month-old) that followed her birth. "It was just God's will," explained Chauncey, whenever Algie inquired about her dead siblings.

Now with four dead infants of her own lying on her heart, Algie better understands her mother's desperate need to hold onto her only child.

Chauncey was overprotective and overbearing while bringing up Algie. Even Algie's father, Berry, stayed at a distance and not simply to appease Chauncey's insecurities. Berry Smith was married and Algie carried the last name of her mother's husband, Willie Jordan. Berry had fathered her dead brother, too, who had been named for both men (Berry Willie Jordan). Algie never knew how her stepfather felt about all this. Willie never said anything. As for her real father, he didn't deny her, but he didn't claim her either. He had 14 other children with his wife with whom he remained married.

Maybe Chauncey thought her chances of having healthier babies would be better with another man. The whisper at home was that she had deliberately pursued Berry because all of his children had been born alive and healthy. The affair only lasted two years; long enough for Algie's birth and her brother's death.

As for Willie Jordan, Chauncey got up one morning, soon after Algie's brother had died, and left him. She could no longer blame him for making "half-done" babies, since her second child with Berry had died, too. The truth is Chauncey never finishes anything she starts, not even the coffee in the morning. Algie used to believe that was the reason why her mother could carry a baby to full-term, but not keep it alive once it was outside the womb. That is, she believed that until her own babies started to die, too. Still, everything with Chauncey is halfway.

Her mother's failure to see things through drives Algie to always go one step further to make sure everything is completed and done just right.

Algie bears no resemblance to Chauncey. Her mother is just an inch shy of six-feet tall with a lean, narrow body that is devoid of fat. Chauncey's limbs, feet, hands, toes, and fingers are all extended to compliment her tall stature. Her satin smooth, snow white hair is waist length and bone straight. She twists her hair into a long single braid that she winds around her head twice to form a tight, double crown. Her dark, cherry brown skin shines like varnish. And despite a mouth full of her own teeth, she rarely smiles, especially these days.

Chauncey only came north because she could never live apart from Algie. She didn't want to leave, but Eddie Mack had made up his mind to go, and so many Clovers were already long gone anyways. Chauncey hates Dayton, the house, and The Place most of all. She never goes to "that restaurant", choosing instead to prepare and eat all her meals at the house, alone.

Chauncey doesn't even venture outside except to occasionally sit on the front porch. She passes the day in the sitting room, squatting in a bamboo chair on an overstuffed cushion. A large spittoon is next to the chair. She regularly spits into it the liquefied snuff [3] she constantly chews. The only time the smokeless tobacco leaves her mouth is while she's eating her meals. She drinks her coffee right over it.

Altogether, Eddie Mack and Algie had six children. Algie had hoped that at least one of them would resemble her handsome husband. But the fulvous beauty of the man she loved must have died on one of the faces of their four sons who were all stillborn. Only Honey, the youngest daughter, has a sprinkling of red freckles across the bridge of her nose, and she hides those with a light dusting of foundation powder.

If Eddie Mack was disappointed that none of his sons survived and that he was left with only girls, he never showed it. He taught his daughters to be independent and self-assured; to standup for themselves and for each other.

Benny has now finished his lunch and tells Algie he'll see her later at closing. She waves goodbye to him and picks up the newspaper at the end of the counter. Tressie brings the newspaper with her when she comes in the morning, and it's left there

---

[3] Snuff is a form of smokeless tobacco called "dipping" tobacco. A small amount is 'pinched' out of the tin and put inside the lower lip. The nicotine works its way into the blood vessels via the saliva in the mouth.

at the end of the counter, all-day, for anyone who wants to read it. It's the second time today that Algie has browsed the headlines and, again, nothing in particular catches her eye. She then decides to go check on things at home, a trip she makes 4–5 times a day.

The 10-minute walk from The Place to the house takes Algie onto Germantown Street for just 1 block. She turns right on Fitch Street, passes 5 houses, and then turns left onto Dunbar Avenue. There are only eight homes on Dunbar (four on each side of the street). Algie's house is the last one on the left, 246 Dunbar Avenue. Dunbar comes to a dead end at a brick wall barrier that is waist high to the average man. A narrow strip of grass separates Algie's house from the brick wall. Down a short but steep hill on the other side of the wall, is a parking lot full of yellow cabs owned by the Westside Cab Company. In the center of the sea of cabs is the dispatcher's office; a wooden stall the size of a telephone booth. Cabbies often climb back and forth over the barrier to Algie's house to place their orders with Chauncey, who recites them back to Algie when she checks-in at home.

When Algie and Edward first saw the house, Algie tried, but failed, to hide her disappointment. She wasn't expecting a mansion, but at least their home in Dublin sat on four acres with nobody else's windows peering into theirs. Chauncey, Viola, and Honey still live at home with her, but Tressie is married now.

On the weekends, Algie even takes Screamie with her during her trips home. She's tried leaving her at the house with Chauncey, but the little girl refuses to stay. "All the little red thing does is scream all the time anyway," complains Chauncey. "No tears. Just screaming. I don't want to keep her no way."

Algie knows her mother's harsh comments are just her way of deflecting the hurt she feels at the child's rejection.

As her feet instinctively walk toward the house, Algie's mind is seduced by the coolness of the clear fall day. Back home its harvest time and her favorite crops are in season; beans, onions, peaches, peppers, squash, and pumpkins. She can see the fields like a beloved painting — row upon row of God's bounty framed by clear blue skies; brilliant sunlight; and splashes of red, orange, and yellow spreading across the trees. Algie lets go a sigh that echoes deep inside her ears. She doesn't regret her decision to stay up north, but it will never be home.

Much too soon, Algie reaches the house and lets go of the fields of home. Six, steep steps lead up to the long porch of Algie's house that has two doorways. The door to the immediate left is always kept locked. Straight ahead, across the length of the porch, is the unlocked door that opens into the sitting room. The main heating unit for the house sits in the middle of the room. It's a large, coal burning, furnace-stove. There have been a couple of cool nights this October, but no fire has been lit yet for the season.

Directly behind the stove are two large windows nailed shut and obscured by heavy, white lace curtains. The curtains are discolored from constant exposure to the stove's ash and smoke. Despite repeated washings, they will never be bright, white again.

Opposite the furnace is a long sofa that is the length of the wall. In front of the sofa is an oblong, pecan wood, cocktail table with straight, square legs that have been painted white. In the corner, next to the sofa, there's a tall, floor lamp with an umbra shade shaped like a Chinese lantern. On the other side of the sofa is a single, round table. The only telephone in the house is sitting on it.

Chauncey's place is on the left side of the furnace. Right pass her chair is the door that leads to the kitchen. It's a boxcar-shaped room with just enough space for a stove, refrigerator, and a single sink on one side. On the other side, there's a round table with a cork top and two wooden chairs placed side-by-side.

Between the sitting room and the kitchen are French doors that open into the bedroom, which is the length of both rooms combined. The bedroom is sectioned off by two makeshift partitions. Two king-size bed sheets are hung over clotheslines strung vertically across the room to create three sections. Each section contains a bed. Twin-size beds are in the first two sections and a double bed is in the last section. At each end of the room is a door. The bathroom is behind the door at one end, while the only closet is behind the door at the opposite end. Algie sleeps in the bed in the first section nearest the bathroom. Chauncey takes the middle bed. Honey and Viola share the double bed. The sheets are pushed aside and against the wall during the day, but put back into place at night for privacy.

To the right of the furnace, flush with the wall, is a radio sitting atop an old lowboy. Edward got it when somebody discarded on the corner of Fitch and Dunbar. The radio plays all the time, but depending on the time of day, music may or may not be heard since the frequency is in a constant state of flux. No one bothers with it, except Honey. As soon as she enters the house, she begins turning the wheel up-and-down the dial. She shifts the radio from left-to-right, until she picks up her favorite dance station or catches "Delilah"[4] to see "what she's talking about".

On the other side of the room, right pass the lowboy is the door-less entryway to the living room. No one spends anytime in this room, except

---

[4] Edythe "Delilah" Lewis was the first African-American woman disc jockey in Dayton, Ohio.

Algie, and only when she's dusting and cleaning. She created this room from money she set aside from whatever was leftover after The Place and household expenses were paid. This isn't her dream house, but this is one of the rooms that would exist there.

The Queen Anne couch and two chairs are upholstered in gold brocade with a deep, embossed pattern of leaves and rose buds. The furniture is covered in plastic to protect it from dust and damage.

The walnut cocktail table is oval shaped with carved edges resembling an ornate serving platter. The pattern in the center of the table matches the design on the outside edges, and is inlaid with a lighter, pine wood. The table has a single drawer in the center and its four legs are carved to resemble Corinthian columns.

On either side of the couch are the matching end tables that came as a set with the cocktail table. There's a table lamp on each end table. The matching lamps have a base and trunk made of twisted bands of iron, sculptured to resemble loose ribbons. The white shades are satin with lattice work edges. Each shade is also covered in plastic.

Doilies are placed on the armrests of the couch and chairs. They are identical; bright white, intricate spider web patterns with fringed edges. Each doily is placed at an angle that suggests randomness, but Algie placed each one just so.

Chauncey is nodding in her chair, mouth full of snuff, but wakes upon hearing Algie enter the room.

"Any cab orders, Mom?" Algie asks, passing her mother on her way into the spacious bedroom.

"I got two." Chauncey calls after her.

In the bedroom, Algie changes her shoes because the ones she had on got wet this morning because it was raining when she left the house. She soon returns to the sitting room and her mother recites back the orders from the cabbies, George and Caleb, who are two regulars.

Algie sits on the couch across from her mother. She leans back into the cushions and closes her eyes. Chauncey, however, is now fully awake and want to talk. "Ya'll busy down there?" Without moving a muscle, Algie replies, "Not yet. It's Friday, payday, so it will pickup soon."

Algie rents her space for The Place from Mr. Frisch. In fact, Frisch owns the entire building; four sides of fading, crumbling red brick with a flat, tar roof. The one level building has three units. The Place is at one end. The House of Faith at the opposite end. And, Clover's Pool Room is in the middle. Crook, her late husband's cousin, runs the latter.

Frisch has been buying and leasing storefronts on Dayton's Westside since the 1940s. Algie has never missed a rent payment, so there's no need for him to make unwelcome or unannounced visits to her restaurant. However, Frisch makes frequent stops at Clover's to collect late rent money.

A rotund, baldheaded, white man who always rolls up his sleeves and uses suspenders instead of a belt to hold up his pants, Frisch doesn't patronize any of the businesses he leases. He just collects the rent and eventually takes care of any repairs the building might need. He knows Miss Algie and Crook are related. But, she's made it clear that the two businesses are run independently, so there's no need for him to question her about Crook's overdue rent or any other goings-on.

The single, wooden front door of The Place is painted dark green and framed on either side by two large picture windows. Honey hand-painted the words, "THE PLACE", in large, bold red, block letters on each window pane.

Inside, a coat tree stands to the immediate left of the door. The Place has a counter that's not quite U-shape. Instead, the counter is open at one end. It then follows a straight line that gives way to a quick, short curve ending at the back wall of the restaurant. The six bar stools are silver chrome with red plastic seat cushions filled with silver glitter. All of the stools have rips and tears patched with heavy-duty, silver duct tape. On a short shelf, on the wall behind the counter, are two, double-burner hot plates; each has a carafe sitting on it. Three of the carafes are full of coffee, the fourth holds hot water. To the left of the carafes is the wall-mounted telephone.

The four wooden tables in the dining area are covered with forest green, plastic tablecloths. Each table has four chairs with intricately carved designs on the legs and rail back. The once high polish on the chairs has dulled, and the warm, rich walnut finish is now distressed. The chairs were obtained at a foreclosure sale and once anchored a very expensive dining room suite. A couple of the tables sway on uneven legs, and the chairs have a little rock of their own, too. Despite the wear-and-tear, however, the furniture is in good condition and the restaurant is always clean.

The linoleum covering the floor has a black and white, alternating tile pattern. And, two sets of overhead fluorescent lights are constantly buzzing on-and-off.

The small kitchen is to the left of the lunch counter. There is less than two feet between the counter and the entryway to the door-less kitchen. The kitchen has a gas stove with four burners and an oven. There's also a refrigerator and a double sink.

Shelves above the sink are used to store dry goods. Pop bottles are stacked in a corner. Perishable foods are in the refrigerator with the bottom row reserved for keeping pop cold. A metal folding chair sits next to the stove and Tressie is the only one who sits there. Just behind her chair is the back door which locks from the inside. Beyond the door is the alley. Two metal trash cans are placed out there on either side of the door.

Next to the kitchen is the bathroom, which has a commode and a single sink. A bar of soap rests on the sink's tiny vanity. A towel rack with a one hand towel hangs above the sink bowl, right where you would expect a mirror to be. A black, metal trash can sits underneath the sink. The room is lit by an uncovered, light bulb centered in the ceiling above the room.

The Place has no waitresses. Customers walk up to the counter to place their orders. A chalkboard mounted on the wall behind the lunch counter lists the available menu items. Customers take a seat on a stool or at one of the tables until their plates are ready for pick up. Every meal is available for takeout on a white paper plate, wrapped in aluminum foil. When an order is ready, Algie hands the plate across the counter to the waiting customer, or calls over to the table for the guest to come pick up their meal.

Next door to The Place is Clover's Pool Room,

which is run by Crook. Algie always uses his nickname when referring to the business next door, never their shared surname.

"Crook" has a two-fold meaning. First, it's short for crooked teeth. Willie's front two molars are turned in opposite directions and four of his bottom teeth are each shifted at a slight angle. Secondly, the nickname would suit him even without the misaligned teeth because of his reputation for scams, cons, and overall stinginess. Algie openly declares, "Crook is so tight he squeaks!" And, no one disagrees with that evaluation of his character.

Although he's her late husband's cousin, Algie has never liked him; even less so, since Edward's death. After her husband died, Crook tried to dissuade her from running The Place on her own, offering to handle it for her. She flatly refused. Angered by her decisive and quick rebuff, Crook began a campaign of ugly taunts, which he whispers or mouths at Algie across the lunch counter when he thinks no one is watching or listening.

"You're slow and country."

"You won't last long in the big city on your own without a man."

"You was nothin' in Georgia with Eddie Mack, how you gone be somethin' now up here without him?"

"Time is on my side. I can wait you out!"

Consistently, Algie turns away from him and gives no reply.

Like The Place, Clover's Pool Room has a single front door with two large pane windows on either side. Nothing is written on those window panes. Clover's is open every day, except Sunday, so there's no conflict with the storefront church on the other side. Working-class men, many of them from the Westside Cab Company, drop by regularly to talk, lie, and laugh — all in that order. The open room has two pool tables and a couple of folding tables and chairs set-up for games like dominos or spades. A little betting is allowed, but the wager never raises high enough to cause a fight or worse. There's no poker games played at the tables. Any real gambling takes place out back in the alley with Crook supervising and taking his cut.

Pool room regulars frequently walk over to The Place to eat. Sometimes they walk back to the pool room with their plates, other times they stay and eat in the restaurant. Conversations started at Clover's carry over into The Place and vice-versa, so there's a steady stream of coming-and-going at both establishments.

The Place sees its share of visitors from the storefront church, too.

The House of Faith has double doors, but no windows up front. The only natural light comes from two small windows situated high up on either side of the large, open room. Each window opens and closes with a hand crank. The windows are open on Sundays to let in much needed air, and to expel a joyful noise into the ears of any passerby.

The church has a stand-alone heating unit placed against the back wall. Up front, to the left of the makeshift pulpit (a long table anchored by two high-back chairs), the Reverend Alfred Peters has a small chamber (really a converted closet). Inside his chamber, there's a card table, two metal folding chairs, and four wooden crates placed side-by-side and filled with various religious books, pamphlets, and loose-leaf notebook paper. There is no window. A small lamp on the card table provides the only light in the room.

In the corner of the chamber, there's a small altar carefully arranged on a white bed sheet lying on the floor. The altar consists of a gold cross, bible, and four differently colored candles. The cross is propped up against the closed bible. Two candles are placed on each side of the cross/bible display. The green candle is for money, the red candle is for love, the white candle is for health, and the black candle is for power. A small basket is sitting a few inches in front of the cross. Each Sunday, before services, Reverend Peters lights the candles, one at-a-time, as he somberly places his written petitions to God inside the basket. After a short prayer, he walks into the main room to begin the service, leaving the unattended candles burning the entire time.

To the right of the pulpit, the 10-member choir sits on metal folding chairs. There is no dressing room or bathroom, so choir members either wear their robes to church or put them on before they enter. Each choir member purchased or handmade their own robe.

The aging, upright piano is stationed beneath one of the windows. The only luxury the small congregation has afforded itself are the six, used pews — three on each side — that fill the room. The church's current fundraising goal is to buy a proper podium and a purple velvet chair for Reverend Peters' holy throne.

If anyone must go to the bathroom before the four-hour service is over, they excuse themselves by quietly rising and extending their pointer finger heavenward. They keep their finger firmly extended until they pass through the front doors and outside. They then walk down the sidewalk to use the bathroom at The Place. Algie has no objection to this bathroom arrangement since many of them will come in and eat in her restaurant after the church service is over.

The House of Faith is all activity on Sunday

morning beginning at 8:00 AM, but is quiet during the week, except for Wednesday night choir practice. At that time, piano chords start and stop while would be soloists search for notes on limited, short-ranged vocal chords. It all comes together for Sunday services, but never sounds like the songs they practiced on the previous Wednesday.

The brick building which houses The Place, Clover's, and the House of Faith faces Germantown, the main thoroughfare through Dayton's Westside. Across the street is a similar brick building with Flamingo's, a nice club for men with coats and ties and ladies wearing high-heeled shoes, on one end. In the middle is Tommy Lee's meat market. And on the opposite end, directly across the street from The Place, is Benny's Bar.

Further down Germantown, there are row after row of more black-run businesses set-up in shops owned by whites. There's a diner opened only for breakfast, a shoe repair shop, a five-and-dime store, barber/beauty shop, a record store, and so on. There's no reason for black residents to leave the Westside to shop or to be entertained, unless they just want to.

Back at the house, Algie finally pushes herself up from the sofa and, without a word to Chauncey, who has fallen back to sleep, heads back to work. As she turns the corner onto Germantown, she sees her middle daughter, Viola, just walking into The

Place. Before Algie can reach the door, she feels the headache already starting — right in the center of her forehead.

HOT OIL
"Aw sooki, sooki now!"

Tressie is in the kitchen stirring a pot of beans on the stove when a very agitated Viola swings her body into The Place. With her choir robe swirling around her, Viola pronounces to no one in particular: "Why do we hoop and holler at funerals like it's the first time it's ever happened? People die everyday!"

Sitting on a stool at the counter, Early turns towards the sound coming through the door. "Oh, Lord," he murmurs to himself. He likes sweet Tressie and fun-loving Honey, but he cannot stand to even be in the same room with Viola. "She's a self-righteous, play Christian in high heels and tight dresses," he's said to Algie time-and-time again. "Choir robes don't cover up no sins and everybody knows none of her boyfriends are single mens."

Most times Algie remains silent and doesn't refute Early's accusations. However, when she's had enough, she shuts him up with a sharp: "Let sleeping dogs lie, Early Bird!"

Algie knows more about Viola than any of them will ever know. Her nightly prayers for her middle daughter are the most intense and agonizing because she knows God knows, too.

Algie is only a few steps behind Viola and walks in the door just as she concludes her pronouncement on funerals. Early is headed for the door.

"Well, babe, I got to went," he says, smiling at Algie before turning to give Viola a disgusted backwards glance.

Viola's eyes flash right back at him and she laughs out loud, while shouting after him, "Mama's baby! Daddy's maybe?"

Many people doubt that Early is Screamie's father. The child bears no resemblance to him or the mother, so there must be a third party involved. However, everyone, except Viola, keeps their suspicions to themselves.

After her unsolicited statement on mourning and death, Viola walks around the counter and pours herself a cup of black coffee — no sugar, no cream. Tressie glances over at her sister from the kitchen with neither a frown nor a smile.

"Did a lot of people turn out for the funeral?" Algie asks Viola, as she takes her seat on the stool behind the counter.

"Oh, yeah. They had a good crowd," replies Viola,

cup in hand, taking a seat on the stool across the counter from her mother. "I was just saying, right before you came in, that all that hoopin'-and-hollerin' was just unnecessary, though. Some people just want to be seen. For goodness sake, Mother Moore was 99 years old! We knew she was gonna die."

"Did Mother Moore have any family left to attend her services?" continues Algie, without looking up from the newspaper she's started to read.

"She has a son, but he didn't make it," says Viola. "He still lives down south in Florida somewhere. He's about 80 years old and his kids are up in age, too."

Viola pauses to take a full sip of coffee before continuing. "But, Pete Farris and her hens carried on like Mother Moore was a young woman in the prime of life. It was all for show, Mama, and it were embarrassing! I know Pastor just about died from the shame of it all."

No one in the restaurant offers any comment. The two lone customers eating in the restaurant don't know Viola, Pete, or the hens. And Algie and Tressie have heard it all a thousand times before.

"Anything new going on at Mt. Moriah?" asks Algie. She's not really interested, but doesn't want

Viola to go on-and-on about the hens and the funeral.

Viola is filling up her second cup of coffee and returns to her stool before answering. "Well, the senior choir is getting new robes, so I met with some of the sisters at the church this week to look over the new designs."

"See anything you like?" Algie continues.

Viola pauses a moment to admire the satin, royal blue, ankle-length robe with the wide, white collar dropping off her shoulders and down her back. The cuffs are trimmed with double bands of gold and matching gold bands runs down the center on either side of the zipper.

"To tell the truth, I like the robes we have now," she concludes.

Viola April Clover (she was born on April 27) is two inches taller than her siblings with an embraceable, curved body that overpowers the petite frames of her mother and sisters. Her skin is always moist as if there is an internal sprinkler inside her body, keeping all her fleshly parts lightly misted — no matter what the temperature.

Viola's long, black hair is styled into soft layers that rest on her shoulders like a mink stole. Her eyebrows are drawn into large, high arches that meet her flat, straight bangs. Her face is heavily dusted with a powder that's two shades lighter than her own skin tone, and several layers of stoplight red lipstick fill each and every crevice of her full lips.

Viola's skintight A-line dresses get her noticed in-and-out of her blue and gold choir robe that she is rarely seen without. The ever present robe is draped over her arm or she's got it on, unzipped and flying around her like a cape. She always wears spiked-heel shoes with narrow pointed toes that, based on Honey's observation, could "kill a roach in a corner."

When introduced to men, Viola looks directly at them as she presses her soft damp hand into their eager palm and squeezes firmly. She never shakes hands with women.

Viola is moody, unpredictable, and selective with her affections. Algie is respected. Tressie is tolerated. Honey is adored, while Chauncey is ignored.

Algie has tried unsuccessfully to get Viola and Honey to work at The Place. After all, she and Edward had hoped to make this a family business. Viola has no job, but seems to have plenty of money whenever she needs it. "Besides, I can't cook anyways," says Viola. "At least that's yall's opinion."

Honey told her mother she wanted a job where she could meet some real people. "Real people come into this restaurant," countered Algie.

"Yes, Mama, but they're the folks with the real jobs that come by here to eat," pleaded Honey. "Like them, I want to be able to buy my own meals and my own fun."

Honey Emerald Clover has eyes like creamy, caramel drops. Algie thought the light hue in her infant's eyes might turn green like Edward's, so she wanted to name her Emerald. Eddie Mack wasn't so sure, and besides, he loved those honey, brown eyes just the way they were. Although Algie had named their other children without input from Edward, she had to compromise on her baby daughter's name.

Honey is petite like her mother and older sister, but with one notable difference — her rear end. She wears pencil skirts that appear streamlined from the front. But with the slightest lean to either side — and she always stands at an angle with both hands on her hips — the back line gives way to a round, firm mound that moves with her, not against her. "No loose ends here," Honey proudly remarks in reference to her shapely behind.

Honey layers mascara onto her fragile, thin eyelashes until they dart up from her eyes like sun rays. Her favorite lip color matches her eyes; soft, creamy brown. She shaves off her jagged eyebrows and uses a thick brown pencil to redraw them, smooth and evenly, back on each day. She wears pumps like Viola, but not the kind with the knife-like point. She doesn't need them. Honey's hard, high calves flex even when she walks in her bare feet. Instead, she opts for a shorter heel, a rounder toe, and a lower vamp[5] to reveal her perfectly plumped toe cleavage.

Honey cuts her hair short, but only low enough to reveal a ripple of thick, dark chocolate waves. Her hair also has a permanent shine that makes it look wet all the time. She fingers the curls around her face to form a carefree, curly frame. She's worn her hair longer, but her daddy's cow licks make her head look a "raggedy mess".

After Eddie Mack's death, the Buick sat in front of the house for an entire year. When Honey turned 15, however, she started up the engine and began practicing driving by guiding the car up and down Dunbar Avenue. She's the only one of the daughters that can drive. Whenever Algie needs a ride to the bank, grocery store, or anywhere, Honey drives her.

A free spirit whose good-natured antics are accepted without complaint by both her family and friends, Honey begins partying every Friday evening with her girlfriend Ruby, and goes straight

---

[5] The vamp is the upper part of the shoe.

through Sunday morning. The first to laugh and the last to stop smiling, "Mama, when I die," Honey declares, "I want you to put on my headstone: 'The world don't owe me a thing, I had a good time!' "

Honey can cook as well as Tressie, but doesn't want to stand over a hot stove all day. Instead, she got a factory job at Woodbine's making motor parts for box window fans. She uses the car to get to-and-from work. Every day, during her lunch break, she calls her mother at The Place, to check on her.

Algie and Tressie share the cooking duties, but only Algie serves the customers. Tressie works at The Place full-time for pay. She began shortly after her father's death to help her mother get the restaurant going. Her husband drives her to-and-from work.

Tressie Julia Clover-Dodd has her mother's looks and her great grandmother's name. She is a mirror image of Algie with a similar temperament and easy acceptance of the choices others make for themselves. Tressie wears her brown chestnut hair in the same ponytail style as her mother's, and her lips have the same kissable pucker.

Tressie is married to Emerson Dodd. Everyone calls him by his last name, including his wife. Dodd works at the coal station unloading coal from the train boxcars onto the waiting flatbed delivery trucks. Short in stature and modest, Dodd was 30 years old and had never married when he met his future wife at The Place on a Saturday night. He wasn't a regular. At the invitation of a friend, he had attended a special revival service at the House of Faith and came into the restaurant afterwards for dinner. For Dodd, it was love at first sight. He decided right then and there that he was going to marry Tressie Clover. Dodd switched his church membership over to the House of Faith after he met her. Six months later, on her 21st birthday, Tressie and Dodd were married.

Tressie married Dodd, but she's not in love with her husband. Although he's a hardworking man who faithfully goes to work everyday and attends religious services every Sunday, she married him because she didn't want to take the chance that her mother would change her mind and up- and-move back to Georgia. And, where would that leave her? Besides, what else could she want in a man?

The Place is open for lunch and dinner Tuesday through Sunday, closed on Monday. The dinner special is $1.99 for meat, two vegetables, and a slice of cornbread. The meats and vegetables for the dinner special are on a three-day rotation. First, fried chicken alongside string beans with potatoes and macaroni & cheese; next, meat loaf and mashed potatoes topped with brown mushroom gravy and lima beans on the side; and third, fried pork chops with baked apples and white rice with butter.

In addition to the special, other dinner entrées include salmon patties, neck bones, baked ham (Sundays only), liver and gizzards with white gravy (Screamie's favorite), and pig's feet. The other sides available are fried corn, corn-on-the-cob, pinto or navy beans, rutabagas, collard greens, fried cabbage, squash, and steamed spinach with sliced boiled eggs.

Coffee is a nickel with free refills and a bottle of Pepsi® or RC®[6] is 10 cents. No alcohol or beer are served.

Dessert choices include a slice of cake (yellow with chocolate icing), peach cobbler, chess pie, or rice pudding. Algie makes the desserts at home, in the mornings, before The Place opens.

Lunch at the Place is a sandwich on white bread. Choices are a BLT, tuna or chicken salad, or fried fish served with your choice of "hot" fries, coleslaw, or potato salad; dill pickle on the side. The "hot" fries are a big seller at The Place and customers can get an order during dinner, too, if it's not too busy.

To make an order of "hot" fries, Algie takes two, medium-size potatoes and slices them into thick wedges. She then places the potatoes into a cast-iron skillet filled with hot oil. When the potatoes are nearly done, she adds a small, coarsely

---

[6] Royal Crown Cola

chopped Bermuda® onion. Algie prefers her native Sweet Vidalia® onions, but "you can't find them up here!" she complains.

When the potatoes are crisp and the onions browned, she scoops them out of the skillet with a spatula onto a double-stacked paper plate and immediately sprinkles them with salt. She then squirts a dash of white vinegar onto the fries. To complete the order, Algie pours a thick, red mixture of half ketchup and half hot sauce onto the fries and tosses it all together using two forks.

In addition to the "hot" fries, the fried chicken at The Place is another menu favorite. The chicken has to be prepared a day in advance. Algie learned the recipe by watching her grandmother, Julia, who prepared fried chicken for nearly every Sunday meal back home.

To prepare the chicken, Algie cuts the birds into four large pieces; two wings/breasts and two thighs/drumsticks. The chickens' innards, neck, back, and any other assorted pieces are set aside and used for making cornbread dressing or boiled as stock for cooking beans. The cut-up chickens are thoroughly cleaned and dried and then placed into a large aluminum bucket. A mixture of eggs, buttermilk, and crushed garlic is poured over the chicken. Algie puts a clean white dish towel over the mouth of the bucket and places it in the refrigerator overnight.

The next day, she places the cast-iron skillet on the fire and drops several large chunks of lard into the pan. While the lard is melting, she removes the bucket of chicken from the refrigerator and drops each chicken piece, separately, into a brown paper sack that is half-way filled with white flour seasoned with salt, black pepper, crushed red pepper, and equal pinches of oregano and parsley. Algie next squeezes the top of the bag closed with one hand, and uses her other hand to support it. She carefully shakes the bag to fully coat the chicken pieces. To check the temperature of the oil, she sprinkles a few drops of water into the center of the pan. If the oil pops and spits, it's ready for the chicken. Algie shakes excess flour from each piece of chicken as she removes it from the bag and drops it into the skillet. When the chicken has finished cooking, each golden brown piece is placed on a paper plate and set aside. To complete the entrée, customers can either dot the fried chicken with hot sauce from the bottle on the counter. Or, they can request some honey in a paper cup for dipping.

The aroma of the frying chicken permeates every thing in the small restaurant — no escaping it. There is never any fried chicken left over whenever it is offered. Some customers even track the rotation of the special at The Place, so they know when fried chicken will be on the menu.

Despite repeated customer requests, fried chicken

dinners are only available as they come around in the rotation. The prep time takes too long and Algie "doesn't want to be cutting up chickens every day."

Viola is now pouring her third cup of coffee. She pretends not to notice her mother running back-and-forth into the kitchen to assemble or retrieve orders. She never offers to help either.

Viola's relationship with her father had been distant. She felt he favored Tressie over her and Honey, just because she was the oldest and looked the most like Algie. The truth, however, is that Edward worried less about Tressie and Honey than he did about Viola. While still living in Dublin, he had told Algie he didn't like the way Viola was "coming along". He thought her clothes were "too tight" and she spent too much time with boys when "she ain't no tomboy".

When they first came to Dayton, Viola was 16 years old. Within two months of their arrival, she was "courting" the 30-year-old, married cab dispatcher, Harris. It wasn't her first relationship with an older man. There had been a couple of others back in Dublin, but her parents never found out about them.

This time, Eddie Mack did hear about it and he confronted Harris at his dispatcher's window. He loudly declared Viola and all his daughters off-limits to the cabbies. He backed-up his threat with a baseball bat, banging it several times against the stall causing it to vibrate. Harris got the message and so did the others. But soon after Edward's unexpected death, Viola was dating cab drivers again, and eventually Tressie joined her. At 14, Honey was still too young for dating. In face, she didn't respond to the advances of the cabbies until she was almost 17 years old.

Although all three of Algie's daughters have, at one time or another, dated one or more of the cabbies, Viola is the most prolific with six.

Not yet married, Viola says she's, "Waitin' on the Lord to bring me a good man." While she waits, she's spending lots of time in the company of older, married men, including her pastor, Henry Farris.

Henry Wilson Farris is the pastor of Mt. Moriah Baptist Church. He's a thick, muscular man who uses his masculinity every chance he gets. When he preaches, the sweat from his black skin shines like moonlight as he prances, wringing wet, back-and-forth across the platform and around the pulpit. Henry keeps a large, white handkerchief wrapped around his right hand to periodically wipe the pouring sweat from his forehead. As he walks, his tree-trunk-like thighs bulge through his pants, and the muscles in his arms and shoulders roll and push out of his jacket. His high-octane voice doesn't need a microphone as he quotes and misquotes God's word from Genesis to Revelation.

Henry's wife, Lillian "Pete" Morris–Farris, first met her second husband when he was the guest pastor at New Bethel Missionary Church. His sermon left Pete breathless, along with the other women who filled the first three rows at New Bethel to get a look at the new, single preacher. New Bethel is the church Pete and her first husband, Galen Morris, presided over.

Galen's father was already a minister when he came north from Ocilla, Georgia. He was the first "ordained" pastor of the then fledgling church. Pete's parents had come north from Montgomery, Alabama. The two families lived side-by-side in a duplex on Danner Avenue. Both Pete and Galen were born in Dayton and grew up together. She was outspoken, ambitious, and more often than not, rude. He was soft-spoken, kind, non-assuming, and sensitive.

Pete always took the lead during their childhood games and arranged all their social outings as teenagers. With his father's influence and Pete's urging, Galen was already a junior pastor at New Bethel by the time the two married, right out of high school. Pete proposed and Galen accepted.

Pete is considered "high yellow," but could never pass. She has a white grandparent on both her maternal and paternal sides, but her eggshell white skin lies over a broad flat nose and wide, protruding lips. Her ash blonde hair is thick, coarse, and difficult to straighten. Pete is very thin and at 5'9" is considered tall for a woman. Her straight back and properly poised head are the result of intense training by her mother, who constantly reminded her daughters that their family "was never field hands". Unlike her younger sister, who got the coloring and the Anglo features of their white grandparents, Pete looks black and, according to her mother, "must work harder to keep her status".

Pete's color-struck parents consented to her marriage because of the stature Galen's family was gaining in the community due to his father's leadership at New Bethel.

Pete and Galen had been married only three years, when Galen's father was killed in a train accident. Galen immediately took his father's pulpit and Pete continued her father-in-law's campaign to "grow the church". Within 10 years, New Bethel's membership rolls topped 500.

The couple had no children. And, there was talk that the pastor of New Bethel had more interest in the young males that flocked to his popular church than in his wife. Despite the rumors, Reverend Morris was beloved, while Sister Morris was feared. When Galen, too, was killed while working at the train yard, New Bethel erupted into a power struggle that ended with Pete marginalized in the new church hierarchy.

Dethroned, she sought refuge at Mt. Moriah and saw in Henry Farris another opportunity to build-up a church and set herself on high. And, this time, with a real man.

When Pete first arrived at Mt. Moriah, many in the congregation welcomed her. They all had heard about what happened over at New Bethel. And since their preacher wasn't married, Mt. Moriah needed a "mother"; that is, a matriarch the sisters could look up to and a "voice" for the womenfolk at the altar. Pete gratefully stepped into the role and, initially, executed her duties with humility and respect towards all. Eventually, she and Henry began having dinner meetings at her house to discuss church affairs.

After one particular meal of smothered chicken with candied yams, turnip greens, and cornbread, Pete sat down on her couch at the opposite end from Henry.

"Reverend Henry," she began. "I know plenty of folks over at New Bethel who are dissatisfied with the way things are being handled over there now."

"That may be Sister Morris, but what can we do about it?" Henry asked, like a student listening to a teacher.

"Let's hold a revival!" Pete shouted. "But not just any kind of tent meeting. We'll call it an 'Old Time Religion' meeting. We'll talk it up among the members and the word will surely spread. Tell them we're bringing back the religion we all knew down South.

"Two spirit-filled days," she continued. "Spirit filled days of down home prayer, songs, and blessings."

Henry listened carefully and paused for only a few seconds to add, "That's a great idea! Many people still do miss their home church from down South. But I'm surprised you thought of that Sister Morris."

She gave him a look that was both hurt and defensive. Henry caught the look and quickly explained. "What I mean is, you told me you were born right here in Dayton. So, you did not grow up in the church down South."

Pete smiled and took time to calm down before answering. She eyed every tendon and muscle on the body of the sexiest man she had ever met. In a slow, level voice, she finally responded. "That's true Henry. But I know what folks want, and oftentimes what they need, long before they even know it themselves."

Henry returned her steady, unwavering stare in

silence. From that moment on, what followed dinner was a different kind of business, but it would achieve the same goal. In a short while, Pete and her clique of women (called hens by Viola and others in the church who are opposed to Pete's influence) were running Mt. Moriah's usher board, women's missionary, choir, Sunday school, and nearly every other church committee except the deacon's board.

Pete's hens include Hazel Fuqua. Pencil thin with transparent skin and a new wig every Sunday, Hazel is easily offended and chronically paranoid. A widow, she wears her dead husband's wedding band on a chain around her neck. Hazel speaks of him as if he was still alive and offers "his" opinions on church business from the grave.

Deborah James is the prettiest of the flock. She's petite with a cute shape made even cuter by her array of tailored suits worn with ruffled white blouses. Her matching hats each have a short veil that casts a soft shadow across her clear, grey eyes. Deborah recently remarried for the third time and unashamedly declares, "I'm going to keep trying until I get it right!"

Next, you can't miss Charlotte Milton's face decorated with thick, blue eye shadow; heavy, black eye liner; and candy red lipstick. She's from Jackson, Mississippi, and still travels home every summer to visit her mother. Charlotte is 30 years old, single, and never married. But, she always has one or two prospects lined up. Finding a husband is her number one priority and Charlotte won't rest until the Lord answers her prayer.

Margaret "Peggy" Linwood and her deacon husband, Boss, have seven children and counting. She's the hens' mother confessor. Boss is Henry's best friend and confidante. It was Boss that encouraged Henry to marry Pete telling the younger man, "None of these young, hot things can bring you the respect or power that Sister Morris can."

Rounding out the flock is Geneva Black. She attends most church services alone because her truck driver husband is often away on the road. Their six children are all grown, but none of them is "saved". Geneva helps with the planning, but doesn't participate in many of the church's special activities. The numerous duties she's obligated to perform for her large — mostly unemployed — family keeps her busy all the time.

Despite their dominance, Pete and the hens are constantly challenged by the bulls, Norma Jean and Gloria Collins.

Norma Jean and Gloria are round. Round heads that bobble from side-to-side when they walk, and protruding round eyes that miss nothing going on around them. The sisters have matching round butts wide enough to set a serving tray on. The Collins sisters' broad shoulders strain to balance their thick necks and oversized heads on their round bodies.

Norma Jean and Gloria are both excessively hairy and daily must shave new growth from their upper lips and lower cheeks. The shaving, of course, leaves a telltale shadow and new hair always emerges before the day ends. Gloria must also contend with a heavy, raspy voice that is two octaves lower than her sister's low, but still decidedly female, alto voice. Because of their close age, the sisters are often mistaken for twins even though Norma Jean is an inch taller than her sister.

Norma Jean and Gloria are 38 and 39 years old, respectively. The sisters overcompensate for their extra testosterone by wearing bright, bold colored outfits with matching hats, purses, and shoes. After their daily baths, they dust their bodies down completely with sweet, baby talcum powder, followed by a generous dousing of Evening in Paris® cologne. You can smell them before they enter a room, and always know when they've been there.

Norma Jean and Gloria press-and-curl each other's hair every two weeks in the basement beauty shop they run from their home. The shop is the source of their comfortable means of living. Their mother taught them how to do hair and they've never considered any other career other than marriage and babies, which has eluded them both, thus far.

Norma Jean met Henry first. He came by the shop to pick up his then girlfriend, who still remains one of her best clients. The sisters eagerly began attending his Sunday services held in the Masonic Lodge on Germantown Street. Norma Jean and Gloria supported Henry financially, domestically, and sexually until Mt. Moriah was firmly established. It was the Collins sisters who put up the cash to purchase the two-story, brick and wood American Foursquare [7] house that had once belonged to a white doctor and his family. Each year, since the purchase, a new renovation or addition has been needed to keep pace with the rapid growth of the congregation. The 350-seat church is now the second largest black church in the city; second only to New Bethel.

Henry baited Norma Jean and Gloria with promises of marriage, which he tossed back-and-forth between the two sisters. The rivalry kept constant fights going on between them, with each sister trying to outdo the other for Henry's favor.

Then, without a word to either one of them, Henry stood up in the pulpit one Sunday morning and announced his engagement to Pete. Norma Jean and Gloria were devastated.

---

[7] The American Foursquare-style home featured four large, boxy rooms with arched entries between common rooms and a large front porch with wide stairs.

The entire first year of Pete and Henry's marriage, the sisters kept a low profile, not participating in any church events, except for the choir. Despite their masculine sound, both sisters have beautiful singing voices and they perform with great emotion and depth.

Norma Jean and Gloria began coming late for services and would leave early before the final prayer. Even many of Mt. Moriah's church members had expected that Henry would choose one of the sisters to marry. But Norma Jean and Gloria were being used and everyone could see that, too — that is, everyone except, Norma Jean and Gloria.

And then one Sunday with only the soft piano keys of a familiar song being played in the background, Henry symbolically opened the doors of the church just as he did after every service. Standing dead center in front of the pulpit, he extended his right hand towards the congregation. In a slow, melodic cadence that is both comforting and seductive, he said:

> *"Let the doors of the church be open." (pause)*
> *"Come in." (pause)*
> *"Help us to build Mt. Moriah." (pause)*
> *"On a true and solid foundation." (pause)*
> *"Foundation." (longer pause)*
> *"That won't give away."*

He repeated the invitation in the same manner several times, allowing newcomers enough time to work up their nerve to walk up to the front of the church.

It was on that Sunday that Viola joined Mt. Moriah. She slowly walked towards the pulpit with her head reverentially bowed toward the ground. Her navy blue, A-line sheath was as snug as a glove and just brushed the top of her knees. White ruffle trimming ran along the hemline, at the end of each sleeve, and created the collar that plunged to a "V" in the center of her chest. Her oversized, matching navy blue hat resembled a pirate's brim. A white crinoline scarf was tied around the hat band with the excess flowing across the back of her shoulders.

When she reached the pulpit, Viola slowly raised her head until her eyes met Henry's. He stopped talking. And, then, in a clear, steel voice, Viola testified before the church and God that what she heard and saw in Henry was the salvation she had been seeking.

The hens immediately begin flapping in alarm; adjusting their Sunday hats, passing sharp glances back-and-forth to one another, loudly clearing their throats, and turning round and round in their seats. The bulls, however, Norma Jean and Gloria, sat up straight in their seats and emerged from their self-imposed banishment. They immediately saw in Sister Viola Clover the answer to their prayers — revenge.

Viola and Henry were lovers before the next Sunday meeting. And, it didn't take long before everybody at Mt. Moriah knew about it, including Pete. The rivalry between the two women has split the church; Pete and the hens on one side, Viola and her bulls on the other side.

Despite the fact that her voice is average, at best, Norma Jean and Gloria made Viola an integral part of the choir. Standing on either side of her, the Collins sisters' voices more than compensate for Viola's lack. Viola accepted their friendship because she needed allies in the church. Besides, being around Norma Jean and Gloria was more like being around men anyway, since they were so hairy and big. The Collins sisters provide Viola with transportation and they had dropped her off at The Place after Mother Moore's funeral.

Viola has now finished her third cup of coffee and announces she's walking home to catch a nap. Neither Tressie nor Algie verbally acknowledge her departure; they are too busy getting ready for the dinner crowd. However, Algie pauses to glance up at the clock and begins a silent countdown in her head.

Chauncey is asleep in her chair when Viola enters the house. She awakens just as her middle granddaughter is passing by her, headed for the bedroom.

"That you, Vi?" asks Chauncey, while remaining in her chair and keeping her opened eyes downcast, toward the floor.

Viola does not answer her grandmother. She despises the old woman who doesn't say a whole lot of nothing, but is always talking against her with her eyes.

"Did you hear me girl?" shouts Chauncey, fully aware that, as usual, Viola is attempting to ignore her.

There is no sound from the bedroom.

Chauncey pinches off a fresh piece of snuff and rises from her chair. She begins chewing slowly at first and then picks up the pace as she marches angrily into the communal bedroom.

"I said do you hear me girl?!" Chauncey bellows and spits snuff into the room as she stands in the doorway, her head brushing the top of the door's frame. Viola is standing near the bed she shares with Honey in a black, full slip. Her choir robe and dress are lying across the bed and she's stepping out of her trademark pumps.

"You think you too good to speak to me?" challenges Chauncey. "Don't know who you think you are girl! I wiped your nasty behind and filled your crying mouth with milk, just like I did for your sisters when you were all babies. You don't have no right to disrespect me, especially with the life you're leading. And ain't nobody forgetting the sacrifices that have been made on that very bed you're standing over!"

Viola, shoes off now, turns to face Chauncey. Her nostrils are flared and her face is flushed fire red. Suddenly! The phone rings. Viola twists her angry body pass Chauncey to answer it.

She snatches the phone off its cradle and blurts into the receiver: "Hello?"

"Viola April Clover, hand the phone to Mama and go back into the bedroom. Close the doors behind you," orders Algie firmly.

"Mom, I didn't start it!" begins Viola.

"Stop!" commands Algie. "I know, I know, I know. Just do as I say."

Viola turns toward the bedroom, right arm extended with the phone pointing directly at Chauncey. Chauncey reluctantly takes the phone. She knows who it is.

"Ain't nothing for you to say to me Algie. I'm going to my chair to listen to the radio." With that, Chauncey hangs up the receiver.

Viola and Chauncey alone in a room — any room — is a dangerous combination. Algie knew the two would be going at it as soon as Viola stepped in the door. But, she couldn't leave the restaurant and Tressie short-handed during dinner time. The phone was the next best thing.

BACKSTABBERS
"Beauty is only skin deep, but ugly goes straight to the bone."

Tressie and Dodd have been married for three years and have been trying to start a family the entire time. Tressie's first pregnancy ended in a miscarriage. The second pregnancy went the full nine months, but the baby boy only lived for 6 hours.

Dodd has a daughter from a previous relationship, but lost track of the mother years ago and hasn't seen that child, a girl, since she was a year old.

The failed pregnancies have drawn Tressie and odd closer together, but inflamed the cold war between Tressie and Viola. Because for every one of Tressie's blessed angels that should have lived, Viola, the "Christian saint" has had her healthy, growing babies cut, bagged, and tossed. At least one of those aborted babies was fathered by "God's anointed," the Reverend Henry Farris.

Tressie never complains to her mother, Honey, or Chauncey because Viola's "sicknesses" are not discussed. Rather, it's her husband Dodd who hears her anguished complaints to God. "On a regular basis, Viola breaks at least half of the 10 commandments. She murders her innocent babies. She steals other women's husbands. She lies to cover up her nasty adultery. She covets every man that is not her own. And, she even does all of these things on the Sabbath!

"Dodd, you and I don't do any of those things," Tressie wails. "We faithfully attend church services. We pray every day. Yet, we can't keep a child alive in this world. And I just found out that fat rabbit is pregnant again!"

Like a flash flood, Tressie's tears plummet from her eyes. She almost drops the round pan of cornbread she is sliding out of the oven. Dodd quickly steps over to help her. He embraces his wife and she leans hard against her husband's chest, drying her eyes on his clean white undershirt.

Dodd feels the same pain as his wife and is equally disgusted with Viola's disregard for life. Tressie doesn't know it, but he's approached Viola privately. He's begged her to carry at least one child to full-term, promising her that he and Tressie would gladly take the baby off her hands. "This way, you can accept this inheritance from God," he pleaded with her. "Just like the bible says, and wash your sins clean."

Viola never looked at Dodd and pretended not to know what he was talking about. She walked away from him, all the while wrapping her choir robe tighter and tighter around her body like she was tying a tourniquet.

Tressie and Dodd live in a duplex at 76 Benning Place. Right now, the other side of the duplex is empty and they're enjoying the peace and quiet of having the whole house to themselves.

Tressie sits down in a white, wicker rocking chair placed in the corner of the living room just for that purpose. A metal TV tray is next to the rocker. On the tray there's an empty glass, her oversized bible, and a faded Watchtower® magazine. She got the now dog-eared and yellowing magazine from a Miss Stewart who comes by The Place from time-to-time. Algie lets Miss Stewart read a scripture and leave her magazines on the counter. Most times, Tressie just scans them, only reading the titles and the captions under the pictures. But one story caught her eye and she's held onto that particular magazine every since. She even carries it with her to The Place.

The April 15, 1954, issue of the Watchtower® had a question from a reader that asked: "Will a baby that dies shortly after birth have a resurrection if its' parents are faithful servants of Jehovah?"

It had never occurred to Tressie that her babies could live again. She always thought that God just took babies to heaven to become angels. She underlined the magazine editor's response: "Although a child dying a few hours or days or even a year after birth may not have developed a life pattern or intelligent memory ... if time had been allowed for these to develop they would have resulted in a definite personality … Jehovah God and Christ Jesus are able to note and reproduce all these latent tendencies in a babe and to reproduce them in the resurrection …"

Resurrection. The mere thought of it takes the edge off Tressie's sadness. She reads the question and the answer over-and-over again. And when Algie or Dodd give her that look, she responds defensively, "It feels like it was written for me. I'm not changing my religion, but I accept God's word wherever I can find it."

There are no advertisements in the Watchtower®[8], and Dodd thinks this is a mistake. He reasons, "They could promote the businesses of their church members, local places, and even their own worship services." Neither Tressie nor Algie have questioned Miss Stewart about this. And since Dodd is only at The Place early in the morning or late in the evenings to drop off or pickup Tressie, he's never met the Jehovah's Witness lady.

Viola says she has never touched those magazines and she told Henry to give Dodd a call about it. She complained to Henry, "Apparently, he has no idea what his wife is getting into and Tressie won't listen to anything I have to say." Henry shares Viola's concerns and has told her as much, but he

---

[8] The Watchtower magazine has been published continuously since1879. To date, the magazine has never featured advertisements.

knows better than to "scratch around in another man's yard uninvited."

Dodd drops Tressie off at The Place and she is alone in the restaurant; Algie hasn't arrived yet. Saturday afternoon is usually slow, but business always picks up with the dinner crowd. Early comes in soon after Tressie and hands over Screamie to her. He only has to wait a couple of minutes and Algie enters the restaurant carrying today's desserts. Early tells Algie he needs a little money and she gives him some cash from the cash box beneath the counter. Early then heads over to Clover's. Algie tells Tressie she must return home for the peach cobbler that wasn't ready when she left, and she will take Screamie with her.

Tressie is re-reading her beloved Watchtower® article when she hears the door of The Place open. She puts down her magazine and walks to the doorway of the kitchen. It's Reverend Alfred Peters. She welcomes him with a cheerful, "Hello, pastor."

Tressie and Dodd are members of the House of Faith. And Reverend Peters knows all about their struggles with childbirth. He has proved to be a real comfort to the brokenhearted couple.

"What can I get you?" she asks.

"Just a piece of cake and a cup of coffee," he

replies. "I was just looking over my sermon for tomorrow and decided to take a break. Kind of slow in here this afternoon, ain't it."

"Oh, it will pick up at dinner time," Tressie replies as she walks over to the counter and removes the aluminum foil from the cake Algie just brought in.

"How big a slice do you want?" she asks him.

"Be generous," he laughs.

She slices the cake and places it on a plate and sets a fork on the counter next to it. She pours him a cup of coffee and takes her mother's seat on the stool behind the counter. Reverend Peters takes a seat on the stool in front of his food.

"How's your family?" he asks, as he begins to consume the cake. "I mean your mother and your sisters."

"They're all doing just fine," Tressie replies with a smile. "Appreciate you asking about them."

Reverend Peters takes a sip of his coffee, followed by a fork-full of cake.

"How's Honey doing?" he asks, trying to keep his voice as neutral as possible.

Honey? Tressie is surprised. She wonders why

he's asking about her younger sister. She tells him, "She's doing just fine. Why are you asking about her pastor?" The question tumbles out of her mouth before she can catch herself.

The Reverend continues eating his cake and does not look up at Tressie. He takes another long sip of coffee before replying. "Just asking. No reason."

Tressie folds her arms and rests them on the counter. She wants to burst out laughing, but manages to control herself and only let out a bemused, "Well, I'll say!"

She can't believe her pastor has got an interest in Honey. Despite how much she and Dodd love and respect their little minister, there's no way she would let him get involved with any woman in her family. Alfred Peters has a white liver.[9] His first wife died in childbirth. The second wife died of natural causes; she was only 31 years old. And the third one was hit and killed by a car. Besides, he's too old for her baby sister and definitely not her type. Honey is a Christian, but not overly religious. She's not a Sunday-to-Sunday churchgoer. And, she won't be giving up the party life anytime soon. Tressie expresses none of this to Reverend Peters. She doesn't want to hurt his feelings, especially when there's no need. He'll never get past "hello" with Honey.

---

[9] In some cultures a "white liver" refers to an over-sexed woman. In African-American culture, a person is said to have a white liver if he/she has lost, in death, two or more spouses or lovers.

Tressie is back in the kitchen cooking when Reverend Peters finishes his cake and coffee and leaves the money for his food on the counter. She hears the coins drop and yells goodbye to her pastor. He returns the goodbye and heads back down the street to his church. As he walks along, the humble minister talks softly to himself. It's a habit he acquired as a boy. To think out loud is to put it out there. That's what makes things happen. Now, he'll just wait and see.

At the house, Algie is sitting on the sofa with Screamie reclining in her lap. The child was nearly asleep when Early dropper her off. Screamie's eyes are now closed and her body is completely limp. Since The Place is not busy, Algie decides to let the baby sleep for a few minutes before carrying her back to the restaurant. She notices that Chauncey has been unusually quiet since they came in the door. Viola hasn't been home, so this isn't one of her post-fight, angry, silent moods.

"Why you so quiet Mama?" Algie asks.

Chauncey does not reply, nor stir in her seat.

Algie looks over at her mother with a half-smile and waits a few seconds before asking again. "Mama, I know you heard me. What's wrong with you this afternoon?"

Chauncey remains silent and motionless.

In a flat voice, devoid of emotion, Algie answers Chauncey's silence. "Well, I guess you're having a heart attack. Let me know when to call the ambulance for you."

Algie lays her head back into the sofa's cushions and, like Screamie, closes her eyes to catch a quick nap. Just as she feels that sweet roll of slumber overtaking her body, she's startled by a hard slap on her hand. Algie sits straight up in her seat and instinctively embraces Screamie to keep the sleeping child from falling to the floor. Chauncey is standing over her with both hands on her hips and a familiar, twisted scowl on her face. "Don't act like you don't hear me Algie. Them papers is sitting over there on that chest!"

Although it had been only a few minutes, Algie is groggy; it feels like she's been awakened from a deep sleep.

"What are you talking about Mama? I was asleep," she replies with a mix of anger and annoyance. "You wouldn't talk to me when I was awake. Why did you wait until I closed my eyes?"

Chauncey walks over and snatches up the envelope sitting on the lowboy. She thrusts it towards Algie. Algie slides Screamie off her lap and onto the sofa. She then takes the envelope from her mother and deliberately moves slowly to allow herself more time to get fully awake.

The return address on the envelope is Dublin, Georgia. She begins to open the letter and discovers the flap releases easily. Chauncey has opened it already. Algie looks up at her mother with more disgust than anger. Chauncey is staring at the furnace.

Algie pulls from the envelope a single sheet of paper that is addressed to her. It's from Mr. Snell. Snell is the owner of the land and the house where they used to live. He writes that he's heard about Eddie Mack's death, the hardships she's faced as a widow with three daughters to care for, and how she has longed to return back home. He tells her to come back and he'll work out good terms for work and wages for her and her daughters.

Algie is stunned. How in the world would Mr. Snell know how to reach her, let alone what is happening to them in Dayton? They were not on friendly terms with this white man and have had no contact with him since they left. And what's this about her "longing to return back home?" Algie puts the letter in her lap and drops her head a little to clear it. She thinks about what this could mean. It takes only a few minutes for one name to flash up in Algie's mind — Crook!

"So, what you going to do about?" asks Chauncey. "I say we take him up on his offer and go back to where we belong."

Algie carefully picks up the sleeping child and positions her gently over her shoulder. As she stands up, she tosses the letter onto the lowboy and turns to face her mother.

"Mama, slavery ended in 1865. Eight years from now, it will be 1965, which is only 100 years. Most people can live 70 or 80 years. You're 78 years old yourself! Therefore, we're only one generation away from the plantation. You can go back if you want to and I will help you. But as for me and my girls, we've crossed the 'Jordan' and we ain't turning back!"

Algie doesn't wait for a response. She walks straight back to The Place, barely noticing any of her surroundings. Her anger is pulsating through the tips of her fingers and toes. Crook is going to find his way out-of-her-business, once and for all. Talking to him is a waste of time, that's why she's never responded to any of his threats and insults. But action speaks louder than words. Algie knows exactly what she's going to do.

Early is sitting on a stool at the counter when she returns. He's come to take Screamie home. 'So, soon?" asks Algie, as she kisses the sleeping child on her forehead and passes her over to her father.

"Thanks, babe. I'll bring her back tomorrow." says Early. He heads outside for a truck waiting in front of The Place. It's his friend Tate. Tate generally gives him a ride and often takes him back-and-forth on weekends to pick up Screamie. Early gives Algie no explanation for the sudden departure.

"Why does he bother to bring her Mom?" asks Tressie, stepping outside the kitchen to watch the truck drive away. "He never spends any time with her. We do. Right here behind this counter."

"I don't know," replies Algie. "I guess he thinks he's doing his duty by picking her up. I don't mind. I enjoy having her around."

"Me, too Mom. Screamie's no trouble," Tressie confirms. "It's just that her own father doesn't spend any time with her at all, other then the ride to-and-from her house. Just seems odd to me."

Tressie turns back towards the kitchen and tells Algie that the chicken is ready for frying. It's going to be a busy night. Whenever fried chicken is offered, there will be a long line of customers. Algie is heading for the kitchen when the door of The Place opens. A well dressed, young man walks in.

Nathan Farmer is six-feet tall and always wears a three-piece suit; jacket, trousers, and vest with a crisp, white shirt, and silk tie.

"May I help you sir?" asks Algie.

"Yes, ma'am. I'm looking for Mrs. Algie Clover."

Algie raises her eyebrows slightly in surprise. "That's me. Do I know you?"

"No, ma'am. We haven't met." Nathan answers politely. "I'm Nathan Farmer and I'd like to speak to you, if you have a minute."

"Is this about the restaurant Mr. Farmer or are you trying to sell me something?" Algie asks, without a smile.

Nathan lets out a nervous laugh. "No, ma'am. Please don't be concerned. I'm not a salesman. Actually, I want to speak to you about your daughter Viola."

Again, Algie raises her eyebrows with a puzzled look.

"Have a seat Mr. Farmer," she says, motioning towards a chair. "I just need to let my daughter Tressie know that I'll be a minute."

Algie walks to the entryway of the kitchen and tells Tressie she'll be in to fry the chicken in a few minutes. She then takes a seat in a chair next to Nathan and says, "Well, sir. What about Viola?"

"Well Mrs. Clover, to begin, I know Viola very well. We've been dating for awhile now. I met her one Sunday after services at Mt. Moriah. Since she told me her father had died, I thought it best to approach you, her mother."

Algie says nothing, but her doll's eye stare is already starting to make Nathan nervous. He inexplicitly begins to sweat and flail his hands in a manner not normal for him.

"You see. I've heard, not from Viola though, that she's with child. I'm sure it's mine. So, I want to do the right thing and get married. But before I propose, I wanted her father's, or in this case, her mother's consent."

Sweat is now pouring profusely from the top of Nathan's head. His three-piece outfit now feels like a diver's wet suit; very wet and clingy.

Algie takes her time responding, but doesn't divert her gaze from the obviously nervous young man.

"Where are you from, Mr. Farmer?" she finally asks.

"Oh, uh, yes, ma'am," he stutters. "I'm from Olive Branch, Mississippi. My father moved us here about 10 years ago. I've got five brothers. My mother died before we came north. We're a Christian family, Mrs. Clover," he continues. "And my daddy taught us boys to take responsibility for our actions. I do love Viola, so this isn't just a duty for me, if that's what you're thinking."

Again, Algie pauses. She didn't know Viola was pregnant again, and she has serious doubts that Nathan is the father.

"I appreciate your honesty, Mr. Farmer. I would have no objections to any of my daughters marrying a fine, Christian man such as you," she begins. "However, you really need to discuss this with Viola. If she hasn't told you that she's pregnant, you can't be really sure it's true. Find out the facts first by going straight to the source, and that's Viola herself."

"You mean Mrs. Clover, she hasn't told you, her own mother, that she's pregnant?" Nathan asks in disbelief.

"No, Mr. Farmer. She has not." Algie replies sympathetically.

Confused, Nathan is not sure what to say next. He mumbles, "Well, thank you ma'am for speaking with me. I'll take your advice and do just as you said. Thanks for taking time to speak with me."

Nathan stands up so fast, he's dizzy. He stumbles towards the door and makes a quick exit.

Algie continues to sit for a few minutes as Viola's third pregnancy settles inside her now throbbing head. She knows what's coming next.

Viola will get up and walk around the house in her nightgown all day long, never leaving the house. Just before dark, "she" will knock at the door. She is the witch.

The witch will be dressed in layers of two — two long-sleeved, ankle-length dresses; two white cardigans; two pairs of white socks; two earrings in a single, pierced hole. She'll wear black, canvas flat shoes and a white floppy hat that she knitted herself. Her shoulder-length hair will be a tangled mess of white, grey, black, and yellow strands of varying lengths. Every feature on her face will droop; eyes, lips, jaws, and even her double chin.

The witch walks everywhere and only stops at a house if she's been called there. Slung over her right shoulder is her black, knitted handbag full of supplies; alcohol, mineral oil, camphor, Kotex® pads, and knitting needles. She carries a gallon bottle of bleach in her right hand, leaving her left arm free to swing wildly as she walks.

The first time the witch came to the house, Algie slammed the door in her face and yelled through the closed door for her to "get off my porch". The witch said nothing, but kept standing there. Viola then tapped her mother on the shoulder, and motioned for Algie to move to the side.

Algie didn't even know Viola was pregnant and she would never be informed of any pregnancies to follow either.

It was winter that first time with a couple of inches of snow on the ground. Leaving her coat behind, Algie opened the door and walked past the witch, without a word, into the cold outside. Algie walked all the way to her closed restaurant and sat there alone in the dark.

Viola was sick with fever a full week afterwards. She downed pill after pill of aspirin. Honey helped Algie change the wet sheets and pour cool water into Viola. Chauncey refused, in her words, to "help clean up after the murder."

Algie walked home from The Place every half-hour to check on Viola. More than once, she paused on her way back from the house to vomit up the disgust, anger, and pain that kept her nauseated for weeks after Viola's abortion. The second one was no easier. In fact, it was worse, because Algie decided to stay.

Leaning against the wall behind the witch, the smell of exposed flesh and blood was so thick it filled up Algie's nostrils. She kept pinching her nose both to block and release the deadly odor. Viola lay motionless on the bed she shares with Honey, pillows propping up each bent knee. Her legs were parted into a wide "V" and a large piece of heavy plastic served as a barrier between Viola's body and the bed she was lying on.

The witch went about her work of tearing and peeling back the resistant mass of tissue, mucous, and life without hesitation, comment, or emotion. Her knitting needles clicked back-and-forth through the birth canal until a heaping, smoldering mass was expelled onto the newspapers stacked on the floor at the foot of the bed for that purpose. A torrent of blackish blood followed. The witch used alcohol, mineral oil, and camphor soaked rags to dam the flow of blood.

The only sound in the room came from Viola's muffled moans and choking sobs. All the while, the top of Algie's head felt like a block of ice, and her feet felt as if she was standing on hot coals.

Algie continued to watch in agony as the witch bagged up the remnants of her now dead grandchild and tossed him/her to the side. She finished up by dipping more rags, barehanded, into a bucket of bleach to wipe down the splatter on the bed's frame and the floor.

Her work completed, the witch repacked her bag and left behind a stack of sanitary napkins at the foot of the bed.

For days afterwards, the "smell" permeated the communal bedroom.

That time it took Viola longer to recover. And, Algie's waves of nausea left her so fatigued and dehydrated that during one trip back from the house, she fainted right at the front door of The Place. A man coming out of Crook's saw her fall and rushed over to help. When she came to, Tressie was kneeling down beside her crying. Benny was leaning over Tressie, and one of his waitresses was applying a cold rag to her head.

"Mama, are you going to come and fry this chicken or what? It's getting late!" An inpatient Tressie is yelling from the kitchen.

Algie gets up from the table and goes back to work.

Dinner at The Place is in full swing, especially since fried chicken is on the menu. Honey and Ruby have just pulled up out front. It's early, only 7 PM. They decide to run into Clovers first because Ruby has spotted a male friend, through the window, at one of the card tables. Their entrance is met with a chorus of whistles and pick-up lines, which they acknowledge only with smiles. Ruby fast-walks over to her friend and is soon leaning against him with her arm draped across his shoulder. He's glad to see her and the two are talking more with their bodies than with words.

Honey spots Early sitting at a table playing dominos. She doesn't wave or head over his way. Instead, she walks over to the low, wood-paneled bar to say "hello" to her Uncle Crook. He smiles at the sight of her and greets her with a loud, "Hey my honey child. How's my favorite niece?

Honey leans across the bar to hug her uncle.

"What you and Ruby up to this fine Friday evening?" Crook continues, returning her embrace.

"Same ole, same old. But I'm a little hungry," explains Honey. "Missed lunch today. So I want to get a plate of food from Mom before we hit the streets."

Honey then turns to look up-and-down at the man that had been standing at the bar, talking with her uncle, when she walked over. She's never seen him in Clover's before.

Bodacious "Bo" Johnson is average height with a nice brown tan that compliments his neat, black mustache and straight, patent-leather black hair. He'd smiled at Honey as she walked over (she pretended not to notice); revealing a hypnotic smile that ends on each cheek into a deep dimple. Bo's eyelashes are so thick and long that women both admire and envy them and no woman has ever been able to resist returning the look in Bo's eyes.

"Who's your friend?" Honey asks her uncle.

"This is Bo. Bo, this is my niece, Honey," says

Crook, making the formal introductions.

Honey and Bo exchange "hellos" and begin a conversation of friendly small talk. Someone at the dominoes table signals for Crook, and he leaves the couple alone at the bar.

"Would you like to go out with me and my friend Ruby tonight? Honey asks, unable to take her eyes off Bo's incredible dimpled smile.

"Where you headed?" Bo asks, unable to take his eyes off the soft, brown curls framing Honey's face like a beautiful painting.

"Here and there. Wherever the night may take us," she replies.

Bo stands up straighter and places his hands in his pockets. "OK, Miss Honey. You lead the way."

"Ruby and I are going next door first to eat," she explains. Honey then adds proudly, "The Place is my mother's restaurant."

Honey turns around and gives Ruby the signal that it's time to go. Ruby nods and her friend abandons his card game to join her.

The Place is crowded. Ten people are standing in line and all four tables are taken. There's one stool available at the counter. Honey leads her entourage to the far end of the lunch counter. She tells them, "I'll get us some food, but let me help Mom and Tressie out first."

Honey walks to the front of the line and asks the waiting couple what they would like to order. Algie and Tressie now notice that she is in the restaurant and they simultaneously nod "thanks" toward Honey. When the line has narrowed down to only two customers, Honey fills four plates with food and carries them over to her waiting friends. They eat standing up and talk about a few places they might drop-in on this evening. A table finally opens up, just as they're finishing their meals, and the foursome sit down. Honey takes away their empty plates and soon returns with thick slices of chess pie. "Coffee or pop?" she asks. Ruby and her friend want Pepsi®, but Bo asks for coffee.

The two couples are enjoying their dessert and conversation, oblivious to a woman that has now entered The Place and paused at the entrance. She stands there unmoving for several minutes. Algie has been clearing off tables and bringing out new orders, but she notices the woman standing at the door. After setting a plate down in front of a customer, Algie walks towards the woman and asks if she would like to place an order? The woman shakes her head "no". Short and stout, she has on a heavy, wool coat which is out-of-place on such a warm, Indian summer night. Her hair is unkempt and Algie looks at it quizzically wondering why she didn't put a scarf on before she came out. Algie tries again. "Are you looking for somebody?" Again, the woman shakes her head "no". Algie shrugs her shoulders and returns to her work.

Honey, who is sitting with her back to the door, still has not noticed the unidentified woman. Neither has her entourage, because they're all preoccupied with laughter and conversation.

Without warning, the woman lunges toward Honey. She then jumps back just as quickly and runs out the door. Bo looks up at the woman and Honey turns around slightly in her chair.

"What was that all about?" asks Bo with a chuckle.

Honey raises her eyebrows and shakes her head in reply.

The group has finished eating and Honey gets up to clear away their plates.

"Ouch!" she yelps.

"What's wrong Honey? Too much pie?" asks Ruby with a laugh.

"No, I just felt a funny pinch in my back," she replies, with a slight look of concern on her face. Honey reaches her arm around to rub the sore spot on her back. When she brings her hand back, Bo jumps straight up, knocking his chair over.

"Blood!" he yells. "Honey, you're bleeding!"

Everyone in the restaurant turns towards the noise. Ruby begins screaming as Honey sinks to her knees. Bo drops down alongside her, but is afraid to touch the wound for fear he'll make the pain worse. Algie and Tressie both come running out of the kitchen and fall by Honey's side along with Bo; the trio forming a protective circle around her. A growing pool of blood is creating a sickening pattern across the back of Honey's pink wool sweater.

Algie orders her stunned oldest daughter to "call for an ambulance!" Tressie obediently picks herself up and runs for the phone.

Ruby's screams have become whimpering sobs. Her friend is trying to console her. Several patrons, meanwhile, have quietly slipped out of The Place, leaving behind their half-finished meals.

Honey is down on all-fours; her head hanging limply towards the floor. She is not crying and doesn't say a word. Bo uses one hand to caress Honey's downcast face, and with the other hand he pats Algie on the back. "Everything is going to be fine," he reassures them both. "I'm going next door to get Crook. I'll be right back."

As Bo leaves, Algie shouts to Ruby, "Get me some towels from the kitchen." Ruby goes silent and just stares at Honey.

"Please sir," says Algie, looking to Ruby's male friend. "Would you go into the kitchen and bring me some towels, so I can try to stop this blood." The man quickly obeys and he and Tressie return with a fistful each of towels.

"Does it hurt Honey?" asks Algie, as she begins layering towels onto her youngest daughter's back. Algie firmly, but gently, presses down each towel against the wound to compress it. Her back hurts, but Honey manages to tell her mother the pain is not "too bad". She doesn't feel faint but asks to lie down. Algie and Tressie roll Honey onto her side and lay her down on the floor.

"Don't worry Honey," says Algie with a brave, but quivering smile. "Remember, you've got Clover blood in you. It's thicker than water and stronger than bootleg wine." Honey lets out a soft chuckle and tells her mother she'll be alright.

Bo returns with Crook and as they open the door to enter, the wail of the siren fills the room. Crook had called for Early to come with him as he hurried next door with Bo. But Early didn't come.

Algie climbs into the ambulance. Bo finds the keys to the car in Honey's purse and follows in the Buick with Crook, Tressie, and Ruby accompanying him.

The knife wound is not serious. "Likely, a small, paring knife," observes the doctor. "It wasn't put in deep enough to puncture any major organs."

The police ask a barrage of questions about the unidentified woman, but no one knows a thing about her. Honey only moans and never replies to the officers' inquiries.

Six hours later, Honey is back at home in bed. Bo is in the sitting room with a frightened Chauncey, who had been asleep when they came in with the news. Dodd and Tressie are there, too. Ruby got sedatives from a nurse at the hospital and Bo dropped her off at home on the way back. No one knows Viola's whereabouts.

As Algie slips the nightgown over her head, Honey, fighting fatigue and drowsiness, asks her mother to "stop for a minute."

"Sorry baby," says Algie. "I didn't mean to hurt you."

"You didn't," says Honey. "I just need to say something before I pass out because I may not wake up."

"You'll wake up," says Algie firmly. "I'll see to that!"

"No, Mom. I need to tell you something now," insists Honey. "I know who that woman was."

Algie gets the gown on and helps Honey lie back onto a stack of pillows.

"Who is she Honey? Why didn't you tell the police? Why did she stab you? Algie can barely catch a breath between her questions.

"I don't know her name," begins Honey. "But I know her husband. And, that's why I think she stabbed me. I ain't mad at her though. I might of done the same thing."

Algie sits on the bed and places both of Honey's hands inside of hers.

"That's not like you Honey," says Algie with disbelief. "You don't mess with other women's husbands."

"No, I don't," says Honey honestly. "But, I didn't know he was married until after we had dated for awhile. I broke up with him, but the word was, his wife was still out to get me because he left her anyway. I don't know where he is. But she blames me."

"Do you know how to find her?" asks Algie.

"Probably. But I won't," says Honey.

Algie squeezes her daughter's hands and then gently lets them go. "Get some sleep Honey. You'll feel better in the morning."

Algie gets up and closes the French doors of the bedroom behind her as she walks into the sitting room full of anxious faces. "Honey's fine. Just tired and sleepy from all the drugs they gave her. Go on home. I'll let you know if anything changes."

Tressie kisses her mother goodnight and takes Dodd's hand to leave. Algie thanks Bo for all his help. He asks if she has a piece of paper so he can write his phone number down for her. Algie hands him paper and pencil from the top drawer of the lowboy.

Once everyone is gone and Chauncey has gone back to bed, Algie sits, still fully clothed, on the sofa. She leans back and closes her eyes, but is badly startled when the phone starts ringing.

"Algie? Miss Algie?" The caller repeats himself.

"Yes. Who is this?" she asks, trying to hide the trepidation in her voice.

"It's me Benny. Sorry to call you so late at home, but I just heard about Honey. Is she OK?"

Algie breathes a sigh of relief. "Yes, Benny. She's

going to be fine. Sorry, I sounded so rough. It's been a long night and I've never heard your voice on the phone before."

"Oh, right, right," laughs Benny. "I hope you don't mind me calling."

"No, not at all. I appreciate your concern," says Algie.

"Is there anything I can do? Do you need anything?" asks Benny.

"No. The only thing I need right now Benny is rest," says Algie with a heavy sigh.

"I understand," he says sympathetically. "Just call me if you need anything. Goodnight, Algie."

"Goodnight Benny."

LOW DOWN DIRTY DOG

*"Everybody who touches this dog is gonna die.
Everybody who looks at him is gonna get symptoms."*
—Chauncey

Champ is Miss Adele's bulldog. She and her dog live next door to Algie and her family on Dunbar. Champ is blind in one eye and his left hind leg is deformed into a short, twisted knot dangling from his side. The dog often hobbles up and down the street, stopping to stiff a trash can or something thrown on the ground. Champ is not vicious and has never bitten anyone. He's never even jumped the brick barrier to go down to bother the cabbies.

As Algie turns the corner onto her street, she stops cold. Champ is standing in the middle of Dunbar with a football helmet on his head.

"What in the world?" Algie wonders aloud to herself.

She quickly decides to proceed down the street with caution. Just then, the door to her own house is flung wide open and Chauncey is standing at the top of the stairs with a broom under her arm.

"Stay back girl!" she shouts to Algie. "Everybody who touches this dog is gonna die. Everybody who looks at him is gonna get symptoms!"

Stunned, Algie obeys and stands still. Her mother is poised for battle at the top of the stairs, and Champ is still standing in the middle of the street.

Algie yells down the street to her mother. "What's wrong with him? Who put that helmet on Champ's head?

The old woman remains mute with the broom handle propped under her arm like a rifle. Champ looks over at Chauncey and then lies down in the middle of the street without a sound.

"Mama! I said what in the world is going on here?" Algie is still standing cautiously from a distance.

With no response from Chauncey, Algie slowly begins walking down the street again. Champ looks silly, but just as benign as he's always been. He's not barking or making any threatening moves towards her or her mother. All the same, Algie keeps some space between herself and the dog, just in case.

"Careful!" yells Chauncey. "He's a mad dog!"

Champ drops his head on his front paws, causing the helmet to tilt slightly above his head.

"Where is Miss Adele?" asks Algie.

Again, Chauncey remains silent.

Frustrated, Algie stops and puts her hands on her hips. "Mama, I said. Where is Miss Adele?"

Algie decides it's time to rescue Champ from his predicament, which she's now certain her mother has caused. She begins whistling at Champ to get his attention. He sits up on his hind legs and the helmet tilts forward over his eyes.

"Come here boy. Come on. It's OK." Algie speaks consolingly to the dog.

"I told you he's a mad dog!" screams Chauncey. "Get back before you get bit!

Chauncey takes one step down the stairs and grasps the broom handle with both hands, the bristles aimed toward Champ.

"Mama! For the last time, what have you done to this poor dog? And why have you done it?" asks Algie.

"He's got rabies!" cries Chauncey. "That's why I got Eddie Mack's old helmet and slammed it on his head to keep him from biting somebody."

The helmet had belonged to Edward. However, he never actually played football. Most times the men in Dublin played softball. But one evening he brought the football helmet home. Algie can't even remember how Edward came to own it. He placed it on their front porch near his chair. And there the helmet remained until he tossed it in the car the day they began the trip north.

"How did you get the helmet on his head?" asks Algie.

"I snuck up behind him," begins Chauncey. "I slapped him across the behind with this broom and he fell over. Then, I straddled him and rammed the helmet on his head."

Poor, poor dog, thought Algie. This crazy, old woman has got nothing better to do than terrorize a crazy, old dog.

"Mama, why do you think he's got rabies?" asks Algie wearily.

Chauncey flips the broom and points the handle towards Champ's rear end. "Look at his backside! The fur is completely eaten up with it!"

Algie is no longer apprehensive or afraid. She quickly walks over to Champ and leans over to look at the dog's butt. It was true, he has huge bald spots. And what little fur remains is brittle and discolored.

Algie looks up at her mother and asks, "Mama, why didn't you get one of the cabbies to help you? He could have bitten you out here in the street."

"I don't need no help," insists Chauncey. "I can take care of myself!"

Algie walks around the dog to get a better look. Champ rolls his head towards her and emits a soft whimper.

"Take it easy boy," she says. "Just let me get a closer look." Algie puts both hands on her hips and stares down at Champ's bald spots. She looks up at her mother again, but this time with a frown. "Mama, this ain't rabies! This dog has got the mange[10]."

Suddenly, they hear a loud noise coming from the house next door! Both women look over and see Miss Adele running down her stairs toward Algie and Champ.

"What's the matter? Is Champ hurt?" Miss Adele's voice is full of grief and fear.

"He's OK, Miss Adele," Algie reassures her. "Champ is just fine. My mother gets confused and acts before she thinks. Can you hold him so I can get this helmet off his head?"

Miss Adele bends down and places both her arms firmly and lovingly around Champ. Algie is able

---

[10] Mange is a parasitic (mites) skin infection among animals that causes hair loss and itching. The disease is not contagious.

to easily remove the helmet from the relieved dog's head.

"Miss Adele, do you know your dog has mange?" Algie asks.

"Yes, I do," replies Miss Adele pointing at Champ's backside. "I got some ointment to put on it. Is that why ya'll put a helmet on his head?"

"I'm afraid so," says an embarrassed Algie. "My mother thought he had rabies."

"Rabies! No! No! Champ ain't got no rabies," insists Miss Adele. "He ain't foaming at the mouth or running up-and-down the street in a cold sweat!"

Miss Adele releases Champ and he hobbles as fast as he can pass the women, up the stairs, and into the open front door his mistress left open.

"Sorry, Miss Adele. It was a bad mistake," Algie apologizes. "Glad you got medicine for Champ. Hope he's better real soon."

"It's alright Algie," says Miss Adele, looking over at Chauncey with an amused smile. "But next time, just come get me if you think something's wrong with him. I'll take care of it. I'll take care of it right away."

"Yes, Miss Adele," Algie promises. "I surely will."

Miss Adele returns to her house and Algie heads for the stairs, helmet in hand. During this entire exchange, Chauncey has stood frozen like a bronze, lawn statue.

Algie walks past her mother without another word. She returns the helmet to its place on the porch and goes into the house. A few minutes later, Chauncey follows. She puts the broom back in the kitchen and takes her seat near the furnace. Chauncey pinches a big pile of snuff from her tin and lies back in her chair, closing her eyes. "I still say it's the rabies," she blurts out into the empty room. Algie is back in the bedroom and pretends not to hear her.

When Algie returns to The Place, Tressie is feeling sick and asks if it's alright if she leaves early. Dodd can't pick her up until he gets off, but she wants to go around to the house and lie down until then. Algie tells her to go ahead, she can handle things here.

As Tressie is leaving through the front door, a non-descript black sedan pulls up and parks right in front of Clover's. It's early in the afternoon, so there are only a couple of guys inside, sitting at the far table playing dominoes. The two white men, in matching charcoal grey suits, walk nonchalantly into the pool room as if it they are regulars. The men at the dominoes table look up from their game. Crook is at his little bar, his back to the men, lining up clean glasses along a shelf.

"Willie Clover?" The older of the two men is the first to speak.

Crook turns around and is surprised to see white men in his place. Even Frisch stands outside when he comes by.

"Yes. I'm Willie Clover. What can I do for you gentlemen?"

"Just need to ask you a few questions." The older man continues to lead the conversation.

Crook leaves the remaining glasses on the bar counter and turns to face the two men.

"Sure, sure. How can I help you?" asks Crook, with a slight tremble in his voice.

The younger man leans against the bar, while the older man begins the interrogation. "How long you been running this place, Mr. Clover?"

"About six years now," replies Crook. "I haven't had any trouble here. May I ask who you are and why you gentlemen need to know that?"

The two agents ignore his questions.

"How many employees do you have?" The younger man poses this question.

Crook does not immediately answer. These aren't cops, but they're sure trying to act like they are. His mind is racing. Who are these guys? He's paid Frisch for the month and, besides, the old cracker has never sent anyone else to collect his rent money. Crook takes a few minutes to calm his rattled nerves and decides to do a little fishing of his own.

"Who are ya'll with sir?" he asks. "Are you with the police?"

The two men glance at each other, and the younger agent stands up from the bar.

"No, Mr. Clover we aren't," replies the younger man. "But we're with the government."

"Really? Which outfit you with?" inquires Crook, his tone growing bolder with each word.

Again, the men glance at each other.

"We just want to ask you a few questions, Mr. Clover. There's no reason for you to get defensive," says the older man.

"I just want to know what this is all about," demands Crook, his voice louder and stronger. "I pay my rent and I run a clean, quiet place. I'm not defensive. I just need to know why ya'll here, so I can tell you what you want to know." Crook is almost shouting.

The older agent steps closer towards Crook. He uses both hands to motion for him to calm down. The agent then places his hands, palms down, on the bar. In a loud whisper he asks, "Mr. Clover, do you serve liquor in here?"

So, that's it. Who told it? Crook wonders. There was no way he could hide the bottles now. He needed to think and think quickly.

"Like I said, sirs. I run a clean place." Crook softens his tone and lowers his voice. "I think we can handle this in an easy, quiet way."

"Do you serve liquor in here, Mr. Clover?" The younger agent, who is now standing next to his partner, repeats the question.

Perspiration is beading up on Crook's forehead. His hands are wet and he's fighting the urge to run out the back door.

"Mind if we have a look?" asks the older agent, as he walks around the counter.

Crook steps aside and says nothing.

The agent bends down and counts the bottles.

"Mr. Clover, do you know it's illegal to sell liquor without a license?" he asks.

Crook remains mute. He looks from the older agent over to the younger man.

"We're going to have to shut you down," announces the junior agent.

Suddenly, all three men are startled to hear a chair hit the floor. The two domino players have abandoned their game. They're cursing and wrestling each other as they squeeze, sideways, through the front door.

"Gentlemen, surely we can work this out?" Crook is almost pleading. Sweat is now pouring down his face.

"And, how would we do that, Mr. Clover?" asks the older agent.

"W-w-well, what I mean is," Crook is stuttering. "I-I-I contribute to the community and I-I-I provide a place for working mens to enjoy themselves without getting into any trouble. I don't want my place shut down. What's it gonna take?"

Both men look down at the counter and then, simultaneously, look up to stare at Crook.

"Are you trying to bribe us?" asks the younger man.

Crook doesn't know what to say. The only sound interrupting the silence is the ticking clock on the wall.

The older agent, again, is the first to speak. "Yes, or no. Are you offering us a bribe, Mr. Clover?"

Crook is caught. Are they going for it or are they setting him up for more charges? He stares at the bar counter and wipes his soaking wet palms back-and-forth across the top. "I guess that's up to you," he finally responds.

Once more, silence dominates the room.

The younger agent clicks his teeth and his partner follows him to the middle of the room. The two speak softly to one another and Crook doesn't even bother to try and hear what they're saying. After several minutes, the older agent walks back over to the counter; the younger man stands directly behind him.

"We're not extortionists, Mr. Clover," he begins. "We provide a public service. Therefore, we're going to give you an opportunity to purchase a license directly from us."

Crook understands the game now. "How long is

this license good for?" he asks.

"About three months, Mr. Clover. You'll need to renew it every three months," explains the younger agent.

Crook looks directly at the two men. He slowly nods his head, sealing the deal on the shakedown.

The younger man is already at the door. At the same time, four cabbies are coming into Clover's. All stare with concern and curiosity at the two white men.

"We'll get back in-touch with you soon, Mr. Clover," yells the older agent, as the two men leave the poolroom.

"What was that all about?" asks one of the cabbies.

"Nothing man," replies Crook. "They work for Frisch, the man that owns this building. They was talking about some renovations and what it would cost."

His answer satisfies the men, and the four of them sit down for a game of dominos.

Crook pulls a towel from behind the counter and dries the sweat from his face, neck, and hands. He wonders: Who told on me? Not the fellows, my stuff's cheaper than Benny's across the street. Not

Frisch. He never even comes into my place. Another thought abruptly crosses his mind, who else are they trying to shake down? Benny? Flamingo's? Algie?

"I'm going next door for a minute!" he shouts at the card players, as he heads out the door.

Algie barely looks up as Crook comes into The Place. She's working a crossword puzzle in the newspaper. She saw the cars and the white men through the window when they arrived. And, Algie already knows why they were there.

In an almost childlike voice, Crook asks, "Algie? Did those white men come in here?"

"No, Crook. They did not," she replies, without looking up from the newspaper. "What did they want?"

"Nothing, nothing," he answers. "Something about renovations Frisch wants to do. They didn't say nothing to you about it?"

"No, Crook they didn't," replies Algie, still not looking up at him. "What kind of renovations is Mr. Frisch planning to do? What's it going to cost?"

"I-I-I don't know, they didn't say," says Crook with a stutter. "I was just checking to see what they said to you?"

Algie finally looks up at the nervous, crooked man standing across the counter from her. In a strong, dismissive tone she replies, "Like, I said. They didn't come in here."

Crook looks into Algie's intense, empty stare. He can never tell what she's thinking, or if she's lying or being truthful?

He walks out of The Place without a goodbye and crosses the street, headed for Benny's Bar.

In the white space above her puzzle, Algie writes the words: NOW MAYBE YOU WILL STAY OUT OF MY BUSINESS!

Before she can get back to her crossword, however, Early comes through the door.

"Hey babe! What's new?" he says with a broad smile. Algie immediately goes to pour him a cup of coffee. "How was the job?" she asks.

"OK. Nothing much," says Early. "He just wanted some sticks and leaves cleared from his backyard."

Algie places the cup in front of Early and he begins sipping the hot coffee. Algie resumes working her puzzle until she hears a soft sizzle coming from the kitchen, just as Benny comes through the door.

"Afternoon Algie," he calls with a wave and a broad smile.

Algie acknowledges his greeting with an equally as broad smile. Before Benny can say more, she hurries into the kitchen to see what might be spilling over on the stove.

"You ready for lunch Benny?" Algie yells to him from the kitchen.

"Yes, sure," replies Benny. "But what I really came over here for was to talk to you about Crook. He just left my place."

"Yes, I know. He was just over here, too," says Algie. "He said two white men came into the pool room to discuss some renovations Frisch is planning for the building."

As Algie prepares Benny's lunch, Benny and Early ignore each other. They listen in silence as Algie works in the kitchen. Within a few minutes, she returns with Benny's lunch, a decision he always leaves up to her. This time it's a BLT sandwich, an order of "hot" fries, and a cold bottle of RC®.

Benny wants to discuss Crook's visitors, but not with Early around. Algie wants to talk, too, but will wait for Early to leave as well.

The smiles and glances between Algie and Benny have not gone unnoticed by Early. Although he continues sipping his coffee, pretending to ignore them, he's angry that she didn't offer him lunch, too.

Benny decides to eat in silence and wait for Early to leave. He thinks to himself: "Maybe this fool will be gone by the time I finish my food."

A new Watchtower® magazine is lying on the counter. Miss Stewart came by The Place this morning. The magazine is opened to a page titled, "Did not Lucifer become Satan the Devil, according to Isaiah 14:12?"

Early picks up the magazine and looks at the question. He recognizes the names Lucifer and Satan, but he doesn't know who Isaiah might be. To no one in particular, he says, "God made Satan for a reason and folks just need to 'cept that."

Benny licks the sweet, hot sauce from his fries off his fingers and replies back to no one in particular, "God did not create Satan. The devil created himself."

Algie doesn't stir. She has returned to her crossword puzzle and ignores both comments. However, she isn't concentrating. She wants Early to finish his coffee and go next door to Crook's, which is what he normally does. She needs to talk to Benny about the men who came to Crook's place earlier.

Early slurps the last drop of his coffee and turns in his seat to face Benny. "God made the devil so people would know what's good and what's evil!"

he states emphatically.

Benny pulls a paper napkin from the dispenser and wipes his hands clean. He turns in his seat towards Early.

"People do not need Satan in order to tell the difference between good and bad," Benny explains, using a precise, affected tone. "Adam and Eve did that for us."

"Mister Thomas," continues Early, trying to mimic Benny's voice. "It says in the bible that the Devil showed Adam and Eve right from wrong when he got her to eat that apple in the Garden of Eden."

"If you could *read* the Bible, Mr. Bird," Benny continues. "You would know that it was the tree in the middle of the Garden of Eden that taught Adam and Eve, good from evil. It was called the tree of the knowledge of good and bad. Satan or no Satan, if Adam and Eve stayed away from the tree, then that was good. If they ate from the tree, then that was bad."

Early caught Benny's dig. True, he's had little schooling, but the Bible is one book Early feels he knows a little something about. The slight doesn't go unnoticed by Algie either. She gives Benny a firm look and slightly shakes her head at him. But even that's too much for Benny! He can deal with Early's ignorance, but how can Algie sit here and defend this dunce, who uses her as an unpaid babysitter.

"If Satan hadn't of spoke to Eve," counters Early, his voice rising. "They would never had touched the tree! So, the devil is still the reason they learnt right from wrong."

Algie has had enough. She slides the magazine off the counter into her lap. She hopes the gesture will end the conversation that is obviously more fight than real disagreement.

"No sir, Mr. Bird," says Benny, beginning his counterargument. "The tree was there first! Satan came later. The devil may be a killer, but Adam and Eve committed suicide."

"Let me get you another cup of coffee Early," says Algie, a little too loudly, trying to distract both men and stop this escalating argument.

Early ignores her and walks over to Benny's stool.

"Who died and put you in-charge of the bible, 'Reverend' Thomas?" Early asks, sarcastically. "Last time I checked, you was a saloon owner and I don't see no bibles sittin' on them tables across the street in your church!"

Benny slams his fist down on the counter and stands up to face Early. The two are standing so close, Early can smell the bacon on Benny's breath, and Benny can smell the coffee odor coming from Early's mouth.

"At least I own something and have a regular job!" says Benny, pushing out his chest. "At least I'm not sitting around here in this woman's restaurant waiting for a job to come to me!"

Early jerks his head to the side and flashes a tight smile, pressing down so hard on his teeth his gums are beginning to hurt. But before he can answer, Algie throws her body across the counter right between the two men.

Startled, both men step back to allow her room. Early bursts out laughing, but Benny drops his head in shame.

"That's enough!" she shouts. "That's enough!"

Algie is completely stretched out across the counter with both hands grasping the opposite end. She turns to address Early first. "Early Bird, don't you need to go next door?"

Early stops laughing and looks down at Algie. Her remark stings and the hurt shows in his eyes. He feels like a little boy whose mother has just told him to excuse himself from the dinner table. Early turns away from Algie and Benny and leaves The Place, without looking back.

Still lying across the bar, she now turns to face Benny.

"Benny Thomas, was that really necessary?"

Benny doesn't answer her. He sits back down and begins to finish eating his now cold bacon sandwich. Algie slides down off the counter and back onto her stool.

Benny takes a couple of long swigs from his bottle, and then pushes the plate and pop to the side. The thing that upsets him the most is that she would defend that no-a-count Negro. He folds his arms across his chest and stares at the wall behind her.

Algie knows Benny is upset, but she needs to talk to him about the white men that were just over at Crook's. She pours two cups of coffee and places one cup in front of Benny, who pretends not to notice. She then sits down on her stool across from him and begins drinking her coffee. After a few minutes, he, too, begins to drink from his cup.

Algie is the first to finally speak. "What did Crook tell you about the two white men?"

Benny drinks the last of his coffee and sets the empty cup on the counter. "Not much. Just wanted to know if they had come by my place?" he replies. "Did they come over here?"

"No, they didn't," she replies. "I told Crook they didn't come over here. Did he tell you what they wanted?"

"Nope. But, I get the feeling he's scared of something." offers Benny. "He said somebody is talking out-of-turn and putting his business in the street. He really was just mostly rambling. I didn't know what he was talking about."

Algie shrugs and returns to the kitchen. Benny sits on the stool for a few minutes more, and then he returns to his bar across the street.

Benny and Early have never argued. The two have kept a respectful distance from each other. Early knows Benny is at The Place all the time; enough folks have told him about it. At first, that didn't bother him too much. After all, Benny's bar is across the street and The Place is the closest restaurant. But, when he found out Benny was walking Algie home in the evenings, Early became angry and he asked Algie about it. To his surprise, she didn't deny it or even try to hide it.

True, their relationship is different. But there are certain rules every couple should abide by and he told her so. Algie just listened in silence, like she does during most of their conversations. She gave him no reassurances and did not tell him that she would not allow Benny to see her home in the evenings. Early thought she would ask him to do it, but she didn't ask. And, he didn't offer. The truth is, he can't walk her home. He's working then, out back behind Crook's. Algie doesn't know about it and doesn't need to know, as far as he sees it. She gets most of what's left of his government check after rent and money for Screamie's mother. He feels that's more than enough for babysitting on the weekends.

By that evening, a few customers are dining in at The Place, but many more are picking up orders to-go. It's busy, but not all at once, so Algie can handle it alone without Tressie who has gone on home with Dodd. She propped the doors open to let in some much needed air, since it's been unseasonably warm this fall. In fact, she hasn't had to pull out the two space heaters they use to warm the dining area at all.

It's Wednesday evening, so the House of Faith is open for choir practice. In between customers, Algie listens to the chords stop-and-start as the choir rehearses for Sunday. The song she now hears is familiar and it reminds her of Dublin. She begins softly singing along.

Do you have good religion?
(chorus): Certainly, Lord.
Do you have good religion?
(chorus): Certainly, Lord.
Do you have good religion?
(chorus): Certainly, Lord. Certainly. Certainly.
Certainly Looord!

Algie's maternal grandmother Julia was the main soloist at the little, one-room church in the small, farming community of Lamb's District in Johnson County, Georgia. Chauncey would sometimes allow her mother to take Algie to church, but she would never attend herself. Grandma Julia told Chauncey it was a sin to blame God for her dead babies. Chauncey told her mother to pray for her, because she wouldn't be coming to church to pray for herself.

Algie enjoyed going to church with Grandma Julia who was well respected, popular, and had a beautiful singing voice. Algie laughs to herself remembering that the name of the church was longer than the front door: "Church of the Rock of His Blessed Pasturage of the Lamb's Eternal Light".

Grandma Julia hated that name and thought it was too showy. She just called the church Lamb's Light, as did the rest of the 40-odd church members. Only the church's self-anointed and self-appointed pastor used the entire name, which he claims came to him in a dream.

Grandma Julia's other children did attend the church; Marcella, Florence, Joseph, Tressie, Gabriel, Charlie, and Ezra. Chauncey was born between Charlie and Ezra and was appropriately nicknamed "Baby Sis" by her family. All of them are dead now, except for Chauncey, of course, and Uncle Gabriel. Gabriel is 84 years old and still lives down South in Dublin.

Algie has a multitude of cousins and recalls many happy times gathering with them for birthdays, holidays, and summer picnics. A few are still back in Georgia, but most of them have come north, too.

Unfortunately, none of her relatives have relocated to Dayton. The majority of her cousins went to Detroit, others went to New York, and Uncle Ezra's kids are all in California. Algie only hears from her cousin Georgia, one of Aunt Florence's daughters, who now lives in Detroit. Georgia sends a Christmas card every year and never misses Algie's birthday on July 18th. In kind, Algie returns the favor, never forgetting to send a card for Georgia's birthday or a note during the holidays.

Algie's thoughts are interrupted when the familiar song she now hears coming from the House of Faith is being sung by a familiar voice. She again begins to sing along; filling in the places the soloist has forgotten or doesn't know.

> *If every you need him, just pray.*
> (chorus): Just pray.
> *He'll lead you and, uhm, uhm, the way.*
> (chorus): Show you the way.
> *Whenever you have doubts*
> *And don't know what life's all about*
> *Call on God to uhm, uhm...*
> (chorus): Save the day.

Algie is annoyed. It's such a beautiful song. Why

can't Viola remember the words? Algie jumps up from her seat. "That's Viola!" she shouts out loud. She looks around the restaurant and sees a solitary customer sitting at a table finishing up his meal. Algie walks over to him. She tells him she needs to step out for a minute, but if he doesn't mind, "Would you let any customer that comes in know I'll be right back in a minute?" The man is agreeable; he's in no hurry.

Algie rushes out The Place and down the street. The doors of the church are standing wide open, so she walks right in to see Viola swaying from side-to-side in her choir robe, trying to finish her solo. Algie takes a seat and waits for her to finish.

Viola's voice is not exceptional, but the tone is pleasant enough. She stumbles over several of the words, and tries to make up for it with a theatrical flair that includes raising her eyebrows up-and-down and rolling her lips from side-to-side with each note. She raises her arms for every crescendo, and then slowly brings them back down like a fluttering butterfly. Despite several starts and stops, the song finally ends.

Algie then stands up and motions for Viola to come over. Viola is all smiles and begins chuckling to herself as she walks towards her mother.

"You didn't know I could sing. Did you?" she laughs.

"No, Viola, I didn't" says Algie with genuine surprise. "But why are you singing over here? Are you leaving Mt. Moriah?"

"Oh, no Mom. I'm just over here practicing." says Viola. "I'm going to be the featured soloist at Mt. Moriah's anniversary celebration."

"Well congratulations! I'm very happy for you Viola," says Algie. "But shouldn't you be practicing with your own choir?"

Viola stops smiling and her lips form a straight, set line. "You wouldn't understand Mom. Let's just say the Lord works in mysterious ways."

Just then the two bulls, Norma Jean and Gloria, walk up behind Viola. Algie hadn't seen them when she came in. She nods a "hello" to both women, who flank Viola like trained guard dogs.

"I was just congratulating Viola on her solo, but wondering why you're over here practicing." Algie repeats the statement, hoping one of the Collins sisters will tell her more than Viola has.

Norma Jean steps forward and wraps her huge palms around Algie's right hand, completely encasing it. "Miss Algie, so good to see you again," she begins. "I know that you're proud of your daughter, and so are we. We're here at the House of Faith so Viola can have the privacy she needs to get ready for her special occasion. The choir at Mt. Moriah is so large and so many songs are being planned. We thought it better to rehearse here. The Reverend Alfred Peters was okay with it, especially since Viola is one of your daughters and he treasures his friendship with you."

Algie smiles at Norma Jean, but throws a hard look over at Viola. What is going on here? What are these bulls and Viola up to? Something isn't right and Algie knows it. She eases her hand out of Norma Jean's grasp and encourages Viola to keep practicing. Algie tells the trio she must return to the restaurant since Tressie left early due to illness. They promise to stop by for a meal when rehearsals are completed.

Algie walks back down the street to The Place with a troubled look on her face. Something's wrong and no good will come from that solo.

When she walks back into The Place, a lone customer is standing at the counter. She apologies for the wait and takes the young woman's order. She didn't notice Benny, at first, since he's sitting on the stool at the far end of the counter. He nods at her and tells her to go ahead, he can wait. Algie gets the order and wraps it to-go for the customer. She then walks over to Benny to find out why he has come back so soon.

"It's too early for dinner. What brings you back so

soon, Benny?" she asks.

Without raising his head, he says, "Algie, I came back to apologize. I shouldn't have argued with Early like that in your place. I know he means a lot to you and my behavior wasn't right. I hope we're still friends?"

Algie walks over and stands a little closer to him. In a gentle but firm voice, she tells him, "Benny Thomas, you and I will always be friends."

He slowly looks up and smiles at her. "OK, Miss Algie. I was just making sure. Well, I need to get back across the way."

Benny walks briskly across the street, but he looks back at Algie so many times, that he trips over his feet twice.

Algie watches Benny tripping over his feet and smiling back at her. He's the only man she's had any interest in at all since Edward's death.

Benny doesn't realize that when Algie first met Early, she intended only to help out a nice young man who was a little down on his luck. Someone had been stealing his military checks and he was having trouble finding steady work. Algie thought he might even be a good match for Viola or Honey. Then, he asked if she would watch his daughter for him one weekend, because he had gotten a job.

Algie agreed and felt an immediate attachment to the toddler. Screamie is the little red baby she had always hoped to have with Edward. Not that she feels her own daughters aren't beautiful as they are, but it had always been her dream, her desire, to bear a child in Edward's likeness.

Therefore, the platonic relationship with Early suits her just fine. Cashing his checks, paying his bills, and handling his mail is all a small sacrifice to pay to have time with Screamie. She doubts Benny would understand any of this, but Algie knows there will come a time when she will have to let that baby and Edward go for good.

TRUTH BE TOLD
"Can't kill nothing and won't nothing die."

It's now August 1, 1958. Tressie is pregnant again. She's in her seventh month and, so far, the pregnancy has been going well. But, as she was walking out the door of the House of Faith on this hot, cloudless Sunday, Tressie felt what she thought was sweat trickling down her legs. Before she could reach the bottom step, the pain ripped across her underbelly and dragged her to her knees. Tressie falls forward and leans against the door of a car parked along the curb. She is unable to cry out for help and barely able to draw a breath. That's all she remembers.

Twenty-four hours later, when she finally awakens, Tressie is alone in a hospital room. The bed next to her is empty. She looks down at her deflated stomach and bites her lower lip, causing it to bleed. The nurse returns to take her temperature and check her blood pressure. Moments later, a red-eyed Dodd comes in and sits in a chair near her bed. He takes her hand, but can offer no words of comfort. Honey comes in next bringing Algie with her. Algie sits in the opposite chair and folds her hands in her lap. Honey stands next to her mother.

Tressie and Dodd name the baby girl, who lived for only three hours, Treasure. They hadn't named

their six-hour-old son, but that was before Tressie
learned from her Watchtower® that they would live
again. This time, they paid for a casket and a plot
at Green Castle Cemetery. Reverend Peters said
the eulogy at the graveside service. Tressie only
wanted the immediate family there, and they all
came. That is, everyone came, except Viola.

It's been a month since the death of Treasure, Algie
works alone at The Place. Honey and Bo help out
on the weekends and some evenings, too. Viola,
however, keeps her visits short and scarce. Algie
hasn't asked Viola to help because the need is
obvious. Viola simply chooses to ignore it. Honey,
however, has confronted Viola about not helping
out at The Place, but Viola always insists she has
somewhere else she needs to be. Honey kept up a
relentless verbal assault on Viola's conscience until,
fed up with Honey's nagging, Viola didn't go home
or come by The Place for a whole week. When she
finally does show up again, at the restaurant, she
brings with her a new, silk scarf that has bright,
green, four-leaf clovers scattered haphazardly
across a white background.

It's early Sunday afternoon and the dinner crowd
from the House of Faith won't come in for a couple
of hours. Viola is fingering her new scarf and
pulling it on-and-off her shoulders. She ties it over
her head and then removes it to make a bow
around her neck. Just as quickly, she unties the
bow and swirls the scarf into her lap like a napkin.

Despite the theatrics, Algie doesn't ask who gave the scarf to Viola. And even though Bo and Honey looked up when she came in the door, they're too in love with each other to notice Viola or her scarf.

Bo and Honey now eat Sunday dinner in The Place on a regular basis. They've been together ever since Honey was stabbed. Bo has never asked about the woman who stabbed her, and Honey has never offered any explanation.

Algie picks up Screamie and walks around the counter. The child reaches for Viola's scarf, but can't get it. Algie asks Honey and Bo if they will watch things while she walks around to the house.

"Sure Mom, no problem," says Honey. "I can take care of any customers that come in."

"And, I'm here too," adds Bo. "How are you feeling these days, Miss Algie?" he continues. "You're working so hard here in this place all alone."

"Thanks for your concern Bo. I feel better about a lot of things now, seeing you and Honey together," replies Algie.

She takes Screamie's coat from the stand and, once the child is wrapped up for the cold, she sets her down on the counter and then Algie puts on her own coat.

Algie finishes buttoning up her coat, and with Screamie riding on her hip, she heads for the door. She stops in her tracks when she suddenly hears Honey laughing out loud. Bo is startled, too, and drops his pork chop onto the table next to his plate. He begins laughing, as well, but he isn't sure why. Algie looks back and smiles over at Bo and Honey, assuming that they're sharing a joke between them.

"Mom!" Honey screams in-between guffaws and giggles. "Look who's coming through the door!"

Algie turns around and can't believe her eyes either. It's Chauncey!

Chauncey is standing outside the door of The Place for the very first time. She's got on her coat, hat, and boots, and she's carrying a suitcase. With more than a little effort, Chauncey manages to maneuver the heavy piece of luggage through the door and sets it down in front of her.

The ceiling at The Place is lower than at the house, so Chauncey seems taller standing in the restaurant.

Viola is cackling like a crazed hen. Honey is laughing so hard, she can barely remain in her seat. Screamie buries her face in Algie's shoulder, frightened by all the loud laughter. Algie is too stunned to move or even offer Chauncey assistance with her suitcase.

"Mama, what are you doing here? And where do you think you're going?" asks Algie in amazement.

"She's finally lost her mind!" offers Viola, as she ties her scarf around her waist like a belt.

Bo is confused and has stopped laughing. Honey's laughter, however, has reached hysteria. She's leaning to one side, both hands touching the floor, trying to keep from falling completely over.

"How did you get down here? Did you walk by yourself? Algie continues her line of questioning. But she pauses to turn and silence both Viola and Honey with a threatening: "Both of you; please be quiet!"

Viola licks her lips to silence them. Honey sits up, takes a couple of deep gulps, and covers her mouth to muffle any remaining giggles. She then walks over to help Chauncey.

"Grandmother, where are you going?" she asks.

"She probably decided to set out for hell on her own," says Viola mockingly. "Even Satan don't want to have to come around here to get her!"

"Shut up!" orders Algie, throwing hard glances at both Honey and Viola.

Chauncey is visibly out-of-breath. The walk around

the corner, in the cold, carrying the heavy suitcase has completely worn her out. She manages to finally say, "I'm going home."

"Ha! Like I said!" laughs Viola.

"Viola April Clover, I'm not going to tell you again!" snaps Algie. "One more word out of you and I'm going to stick that scarf someplace you won't forget!"

Bo raises both his eyebrows and, although his mouth is closed, his dimples are settling deeper and deeper into his cheeks.

"Mama, where are you going?" Algie repeats her question to Chauncey.

Again, Chauncey says, "I'm going home."

"Home?" Algie and Honey respond in unison. "Mama, come around here and sit down," Algie says, as calmly as she can.

Chauncey complies and drops down in the vacant chair next to Bo. She's too tired to keep standing anyway. Algie turns to Honey and hands over Screamie. She hangs her coat back on the stand and walks around the counter pour a cup of coffee for Chauncey. Algie sets the steaming cup of hot liquid in front of her mother and takes a seat at the table. Honey walks around to stand behind her mother's chair with Screamie in her arms. Viola leans back against the lunch counter.

"Mama, what is this all about?" asks Algie, again. "What made you decide to go home today?"

Chauncey is sipping her coffee and clearly means to take her time before answering. During the long pause, Bo sees an opportunity to excuse himself. He takes his plate and coffee cup with him to the lunch counter.

Finally, Chauncey speaks. "I'm ready to go home. I came around here to ask you for bus fare. You said you would help me go home whenever I was ready to. Well, I'm ready to go now."

"Did something happen at home?" asks Algie.

"Don't matter!" replies Chauncey angrily. "I'm ready to go home. Ya'll not gonna burn me up like a slab of pork rib and then throw me to the wind!"

Viola and Honey exchange amused looks. Honey is covering her mouth again to hold in her laughter.

Algie is completely confused. Chauncey has never even left the front yard, let alone stepped foot in The Place. And what is she talking about being burned up?

"Mama, who have you been talking to?" asks Algie, in a voice that is becoming increasingly more frustrated.

"Like I said, I'm ready to go home," replies Chauncey, with no further explanation.

Algie props her elbows up on the table and holds her head in bewilderment.

"Well, if you ask me ..." begins Viola again. But she stops short when she sees her mother's stark, blank eyes fill with fiery anger directed at her.

No one says a word.

Bo has finished his meal and would really like to leave, but not without Honey. He breaks the silence by commenting, "I hate that Clover's is closed on Sundays. I could go over there to get out of you ladies' way ..." But, before he can finish his sentence, Algie stands straight up, causing Honey to trip backwards over her own feet.

"Mama, has Crook been around to the house?" asks Algie, with suspicion and concern.

Chauncey looks up at her daughter and smugly replies, "Maybe he has."

"Mama has Crook been to the house or not!" demands Algie, planting her feet firmly on the ground and both hands firmly on the table.

"Yeah, he come by," says Chauncey. "And, he told me how ya'll planning to get rid of me. That's why you don't want to go back to Dublin."

"Mama, ain't nobody got any plans to get rid of you." says Algie. "Tell me exactly what Crook said."

Chauncey sits staring down at her coffee for a few minutes. She doesn't want to believe what Crook told her, but she hasn't understood her daughter's motives for doing the things she's done since Eddie Mack died. She hesitates a little longer, but decides it's better to get it out in the open.

"Crook came by the house after you left this morning," she begins. "He wanted to know if you had gotten the letter from Mr. Snell in Georgia. I told him you did and showed him the letter still laying on the lowboy.

"He asked me what we were going to do about it. And, I told him it was up to you," continues Chauncey. "Told him I thought we should take Mr. Snell up on his offer, but that you had other plans."

Viola has a smirk on her face, but says nothing. Honey, on the other hand, steps around to face her mother with her mouth wide open. "What?" she yells. "Mr. Snell? You mean that plantation owner in Georgia. Mom, what you writing him for?

"I didn't write to him Honey, he wrote a letter to me," explains Algie. "Now sit down and be quiet, so I can finish getting the whole story from your grandmother. Go ahead Mama. Finish telling me what happened."

"Well, he told me he knew the reason why you didn't want to go back," Chauncey begins, again. "You would get a bunch of insurance money for putting me down like a dog. Then, you gone burn me up into ashes, so you won't have to pay for a funeral. He said you in debt so deep trying to run this restaurant that you took out that insurance on me to save yourself."

"That's not true!" blurts out Honey, before Algie can even respond. "Grandmother, that's a bald-faced lie!"

Algie folds her hands behind her back. She takes a deep, long sigh and then looks over at Bo. "Bo would you mind driving my mother back around to the house?"

"Ahn, ahn, no ma'am," interrupts Chauncey. "I'm going home today!"

"Yes, you are going home Mama," replies Algie sternly. "Right around to 254 Dunbar Ave. Honey hand Screamie over to Viola and help your grandmother to the car. Bo, please carry her suitcase."

Viola takes the child, but promptly puts her back on the mat behind the counter.

Algie heads for the kitchen to prepare a plate of dinner to-go for her mother. Bo picks up the suitcase, but Chauncey remains in her seat — refusing to stand up, despite Honey's urgings.

Algie returns and gently pushes Honey to the side. She leans over and kisses her mother on the forehead. In a quiet, firm voice Algie says, "Mama, Bo and Honey are going to get you back home where it's safe and warm. I made a plate of dinner for you. So, go on home and forget all of Crook's lies."

Chauncey looks up at her daughter through watery eyes. She gets up from the chair, and Honey and Bo help her out the door and into the car. Viola follows them, and Algie follows directly behind her.

"Honey?" Algie calls, as the foursome are settling down into the car. Honey is in the backseat with Chauncey, trying to comfort her grandmother. Viola sits up front with Bo. Honey rolls down the car window and looks over to her mother. Algie says nothing, but looks at Chauncey, then at Viola, and back again. Honey nods; message received.

Algie watches the car until the taillights disappear around the corner onto Fitch Street. She looks in the opposite direction and sees a group of House of Faith parishioners headed her way. Algie quickly gets back to work.

The Sunday crowd is not that heavy. And Algie is grateful for that. She's tired both physically and emotionally. As she is cleaning up for the evening, she hears the door of The Place open. She's mopping the main floor with her back to the door, but doesn't bother to turn around. It's probably a late-comer who is out-of-luck.

"Sorry, we're closed," she yells over her shoulder.

The lack of a response from the visitor makes her a little nervous. She stops mopping and turns around to see a ghost; a ghost from the past — Mazy.

"Mazy!" screams Algie.

She lets the mop fall to the floor and rushes over to hug the equally excited woman who just came in. Mazy is Algie's half-sister, one of Berry Smith's daughters.

While growing up in Dublin, Algie didn't spend much time with her half-siblings. Chauncey wouldn't allow it. But she and Mazy managed to form a friendship at Lamb's Light. Algie is five years older than her younger sister. The girls first met in Sunday school when Algie was 11 years old, and Mazy was 6. The two were immediately drawn to each other and Mazy always insisted on sitting next to Algie. Grandma Julia told Algie that Mazy was her sister, but to keep it quiet or Chauncey would have a fit. Although Algie only attended church sporadically with her grandmother, those few times were enough for the two girls to bond and nurture the natural sisterly affection they felt for each other.

"Algie Julia, you look the same!" laughs Mazy.

"So, do you!" replies Algie. "Come over here and take a seat. How did you get here? Why didn't you call to let me know you were coming?"

The two women sit next to each other, smiles never leave their faces.

"I'm living with my son, Floyd," explains Mazy. "Right here in Dayton, Ohio. I came a little over a year ago, but I didn't have an address for you. I told my son I was sure this is where ya'll moved to, but of course, he didn't know you back in Dublin."

"So, how did you find me?" asks Algie

"Well, Floyd's buddy brought him over here one weekend to Clover's next door," continues Mazy. "The next day he mentioned the name of the place to me. I asked him, 'How many Clovers could there be in Dayton?' He came back the next weekend and spoke with the owner, who told him you were right next door. We meant to come by earlier today, but my son had to work late."

"Is your son with you? "Where is he?" asks Algie, looking past Mazy and out the front windows.

Mazy tilts her head towards the door. "He's waitin' in the car outside."

"Tell him to come in," Algie insists and she stands up and begins walking towards the door.

Mazy grabs Algie's hand and pulls her back into her seat. "No, no Algie. I'm only going to be a minute. He wants to stay in the car."

Algie sits back down and squeezes her sister's hand. "I'm just so happy Mazy you kept looking for me! I was just cleaning up, but I can get a meal together for you and your son."

"No, no, don't bother," says Mazy. "You've worked all day and I've had my dinner. Now that I know where you are, I can get Floyd to bring me back anytime."

The two sisters sit for a moment and just smile at one another, happy to be in each other's company.

Mazy finally breaks the comfortable silence to ask about Viola. Algie tries hard not to change the look on her face before answering. "Viola is Viola. She looks more like him than you, and I suspect she's got more of his personality, too!"

Mazy laughs at Algie's description. "Have ya'll ever told her about her birth?"

"Truth is, no, we didn't tell her," says Algie. "No reason why, we just didn't. And now, what good would it do?"

Mazy nods her head in agreement. "I was just so grateful you and Eddie Mack took her. I knew she was in good hands and would still be in the family."

Mazy gave birth to Viola when she was 13 years old. The father of the infant was a friend of Berry's, who had abused her since she was 9 years old. When her pregnancy was discovered and Mazy identified her rapist, her father abruptly left the house. Berry didn't return for three days. When he did come back home, he said nothing about his whereabouts or what he had done while he was away. His former friend, Viola's biological father, has never been seen nor heard from again.

When the baby was born, Mazy's mother wanted to keep her and raise her as her own. She named the child Viola, after her own sister. But Berry wouldn't allow the infant to stay. Everyone in Dublin knew about the child and how she had been conceived, including Eddie Mack and Algie. During this time, Algie had just lost her second son. She didn't have to say anything to Edward. Algie was still in her sick bed when he brought the baby girl to her.

"I'd like to see her sometime Algie," says Mazy. "And you know I won't breath a word about her beginnings to her."

"She still lives at home with me and is in-and-out of the restaurant all the time," Algie tells Mazy. "I'll arrange a time when I know she will be here."

"Well, let me get out of your way," says Mazy, and she gets up from her seat to leave.

"You just got here!" protests Algie.

"Yes, I know sis, but Floyd is waiting in the car for me," says Mazy. "And, like I said, he had to work today, too, just like you.

"OK. But give me your address and phone number first," says Algie, who pulls the little pad she uses for orders from her pocket, along with a pencil.

Mazy writes down the information and the two women embrace, promising to get in-touch real soon.

Mazy leaves and Algie puts the mop away. She puts on her coat and begins the walk home alone in the dark.

The night sky is cloudless and a bright, full moon lights her way. Algie feels like she's sleepwalking. The streets turn into barren fields, waiting for the first signs of spring. The sound of a passing cab is like Georgia pines shivering in the night wind. She smells burning wood and feels leaves crackling beneath her feet. Did she just hear the night call of a Whippoorwill? Algie can't make the memories of home come to her, but when they do, she doesn't fight them. Instead, she wraps her heart and mind around Dublin and doesn't let go until she has to.

Algie decides not to mention Mazy's visit to her mother, especially not today with all the drama from earlier this afternoon. She is glad to find her already asleep in bed when she arrives. Dear, sweet Honey; Algie thanks God for her youngest daughter, who certainly stayed with her grandmother until she fell asleep.

Viola is on the couch in her night clothes thumbing through a magazine, the clover scarf hanging loosely around her neck. She doesn't acknowledge her mother or even greet her as she enters the house. Algie returns the silence and goes into the bedroom to change into her night clothes, too.

It's not that Algie is indifferent to the consequences

of her daughters' actions, but she wants whatever happens to be because of their choices and their choices alone. She felt emotionally (and sometimes physically) tied and bound while trying to grow up as the only child of Chauncey. With her own girls, she's giving them all the rope they need to either anchor or hang themselves — whichever comes first.

Algie has taught her daughters the practical aspects of womanhood, but she is not their confidante. Each daughter knows that their mother will be there for them through any physical ailment or mishap. But, they also know, she will not intrude on the more intimate details of their lives.

No daughter complains about this relationship nor feels neglected by it. Algie does not ask them: Which man are you seeing? What are you doing with that man? Where are you going? Where have you been? Who are your friends? And, that suits all three daughters just fine.

For her part, Chauncey does not interfere in her granddaughters' lives either. Her focus is always entirely on her own child.

Algie next goes into the kitchen and pours herself a glass of cold milk. As she sits down at the kitchen table to drink her milk, a wave of sadness sweeps over her and she shudders at the thought of where Viola's latest sin offering — the clover-covered scarf — might have come from.

Back in Dublin, Chauncey had opposed the adoption of the baby girl. Eddie Mack and Algie constantly had to shield their new daughter from Chauncey's outbursts. Algie faithfully watched for every slight her mother made towards the little girl. For example, Chauncey would call 6-year-old Tressie over to give her an apple or some other little treat, or pick her up just to cuddle in her lap. Four-year-old Viola would naturally look for the same treat or affection, but was shooed away by Chauncey as if she were the house pet. Algie would immediately take the treat from Tressie and give half to Viola, explaining to her girls that sharing was the best way of showing love. And, she would often stop, whatever she was doing, to sit and cuddle with Viola in clear view of Chauncey. But of course, Algie couldn't be at the right place, at the right time, all the time. And she could always tell when Viola had been hurt by Chauncey.

Eddie Mack deferred to Algie when it came to handling her crazy mother. But before Viola's fifth birthday, he decided to put an end to her nasty remarks and bad attitude toward his middle daughter. His child would soon start school, and with that learning, Viola would become fully aware of the differences her grandmother made between her and her sisters.

Eddie Mack waited until Algie and the girls had gone to church. Chauncey was sitting on the front porch dipping her snuff and drinking coffee. At first, Eddie Mack tried reasoning with her, appealing to her as a grandmother and reminding her of the sons he and Algie already had lost. He didn't expect her to respond to his gentler approach, but he'd always tried to give her the benefit of the doubt.

As the volume of the conversation escalated, Chauncey's body language became increasingly agitated. She stood up in her chair and waved her arms around wildly at him; cursing, spitting snuff, and calling him everything but a child of God. For the umpteenth time, she reminded him that he had stolen her daughter. And, now, she was being asked to accept some bastard baby gotten and born in sin.

Eddie Mack let Chauncey have her say, but soon her tirade exhausted his patience. He let loose a verbal riptide that concluded with a truth she had self-righteously failed to mention. He screamed, "And last, but not least, your only daughter was gotten and born in sin, too, since you were married to Willie when you laid down like a swamp whore for Berry Smith!"

Chauncey balled up her fist and swung at Eddie Mack with all her might, catching him just under the chin. The punch caused him to lose his balance, but he still managed to deliver a slap across her cheek that sent her face down into the hard, red Georgia clay. Eddie Mack left her there and drove away in his truck. He visited with friends until it was time for his wife and daughters to return from church. When they all got back home, Chauncey was in her bed. Algie was worried. She told Edward her mother must be ill, but won't say what's wrong. Algie kept trying to tend to her illness all evening, but Chauncey angrily kept her away.

Despite the fact that, to this day, neither granddaughter nor grandmother can manage to even greet one another without confrontation, Chauncey keeps her thoughts to herself.

Algie finishes her milk and says goodnight to Viola. Viola grunts a goodnight to her mother, without looking up from her magazine.

The next day, Algie decided to truly rest. Generally, on Mondays, she would work through a list of chores and wait for Honey to come by to drive her around town to take care of some errands. Honey works a half-day shift on Mondays in order to get her mother to the grocery store, the drug store, the bank — wherever she needs to go. This Monday, however, Algie just wants to rest.

After her bath, Algie puts on her housecoat and joins Chauncey in the living room. Chauncey is quiet and subdued. She mumbled a good morning, but has said little else. The radio is on, but only bits of music can be heard through the heavy static. Neither woman is listening anyway; a malaise hangs heavily over both of them. They sit for a long while, wide awake, but lost in their thoughts, when a heavy knock hits the front door. Algie jumps up to answer the door. She maneuvers her head from side-to-side trying to see who it is through the dingy lace curtains. She opens the door and the delivery man asks for Honey. Algie tells him that Honey is at work and he asks her to sign for Honey's box. Algie complies and the delivery man and his assistant bring in the large, corrugated box and deposit it just inside the door.

"What's that?" asks Chauncey, coming back to life.

Algie looks at the dark, block letters and reads: Zenith Television. "It's a TV," she tells Chauncey.

"A TV?" asks Chauncey. "What made you go out and buy that?"

"I didn't buy it Mama," explains Algie. "Apparently, Honey did."

"Where ya'll gonna put it?" wonders Chauncey. "You can't leave it sittin' at the door like that."

"It can sit here for now Mama," says Algie. "When Honey gets in, we'll decide where to put it."

Algie returns to the couch, but Chauncey gets up to inspect the box. She can't read the words, but is obviously intrigued by the package. She likes the fact that there will be a TV in the house; it means her family is doing well. Back in Dublin, the first time Chauncey saw a TV was in the home of one of the white families that she cleaned houses for. She couldn't sit and watch the set, but she stole glances over at the moving images as she went about her cleaning.

Algie watches her mother looking over the box. She can see the satisfaction on her face, and then, it happens, Chauncey smiles.

When Honey got home, she squealed and jumped up-and-down with joy. She purchased the TV as a surprise for her family and she's pleased with their appreciation for the big, brown box. Honey picks up the phone and calls Bo with the news. He tells her, he'll be over after work to set it up for her.

The three women try to decide on the best spot for the TV. Their conversation is excited and animated. Algie is beaming at this rare moment that has brought a smile to all three of their faces. She only wishes that Viola were here, too.

On Tuesday, Algie is still in an especially happy mood. She is just finishing preparing a fried fish sandwich for a lunch order when the messenger comes into The Place. Algie gives the teenager a nickel and stares at the flimsy paper. She's never seen a telegram before. As she hands the cabbie George his lunch, she asks him to stop next door at Crook's and tell Early to step over for a minute.

Within a few minutes, Early comes into The Place.

"What you need babe?" he greets Algie.

"This telegram just came for you," she tells him.

"A telegram?" asks Early. "For me? What does it say?

Algie does not read the message back to him verbatim, but informs him that his mother wants him to come home immediately.

"For what? Is somebody sick?" Early asks with genuine concern.

"No, it just says there's a family emergency and you need to get there right away." Algie explains, and hands the telegram to him.

Early accepts Algie's explanation, but is clearly bothered by the request. He's never told her the real reason why he hasn't returned home to Sweetwater, Texas.

Early had a falling-out with one of the bootleggers, a man called Crackers. Early delivered illegal booze to local joints and bars for him. But Early thought the man was too stingy and wasn't paying him enough money for the risks he was taking. So, Early decided to expand the liquor supply and keep the extra profits. He would pick up the bottled liquor from Crackers and take it home to his mother's house. There, he would redistribute the liquor into identical bottles half filled with water and soda. After he had made the arranged deliveries, he would sell the excess bottles independently, pocketing the money.

When Crackers found out about it, he came looking for Early with a loaded rifle. Early took a bus to Abilene, about 50 miles away, and joined the army. Crackers continued to threaten Early's mother and accused her of hiding him and being in on the scheme with her son. Early hasn't been back to Texas since.

Early turns the telegram over and over in his hands. He has never seen one either. And, he wonders who sent it. His mother can barely write, she doesn't know anything about sending a message like this. He sits down on a stool at the counter and silently fingers the paper.

It's his business, so Algie decides not to try to advise Early. She can't tell what's worrying him more, receiving the telegram or the thought of going home. She looks up and sees Bo coming through the door and Benny is with him. Both men are looking for lunch.

Bo and Benny sit at the counter, ignoring Early who is lost in thought. They're engaged in a deep conversation, apparently about a book that Bo has set on the counter. Algie returns from the kitchen, where she's already started Benny's lunch, and asks Bo what he would like. He tells her a tuna sandwich with coleslaw will hold him.

The two men are deeply engaged in conversation when she returns with their lunches. Early has left.

"What's that book about?" asks Algie.

Bo speaks up first. "It's called 'The Invisible Man[11],'" he tells her. "The writer is trying to explain why colored men like myself and Benny are 'invisible' to the world."

"Invisible?" says Algie, clearly puzzled. "You're not invisible. I can see both of you clear as day."

All three laugh.

"No, not that kind of invisible, Miss Algie," says Bo, trying to explain. "He means we're invisible to society. We're not recognized as men, but rather they think of us as stereotypes. You know dumb, uneducated, clownish buffoons."

"Whose it by?" asks Algie.

---

[11] "The Invisible Man" by Ralph Ellison won the National Book Award in 1953.

"Ralph Ellison," answers Benny. "I've never read it, but I heard about it. Bo, here, is like a walking library, Algie. He knows all about all these new Negro writers."

Bo smiles with appreciation at Benny. He's no expert, but he does have a voracious appetite for reading.

"I've always loved to read Miss Algie," says Bo. "But my reading only began to have an affect on my life when I discovered how blessed the 1950s have been for us. There are so many books written by Negroes about our lives, our history, and even our future."

"Listen to him Algie," says Benny with pride. "He sounds like a college professor, don't he?"

"Yes, he does Benny," says Algie in agreement. "And, there's nothing wrong with that."

Algie likes Bo and now she likes him even more. Maybe his love of books and learning will rub-off on Honey. Even if it doesn't, it won't hurt for Honey to be the wife of such a man. Although she can read and write fairly well, Algie has always admired people who can read and understand fine books; that is, books bound in leather and trimmed in gold. This book doesn't look like that, but from what Bo said about it, the words could certainly be stored inside such precious pages.

She takes her seat on her stool and leaves the two men to their meal and their man-talk.

The door of The Place opens and in walks Early, again. Despite his trepidation, he tells her he's decided to buy a bus ticket for home. He plans to leave on Wednesday or Thursday and should be back in a week.

Benny is still facing Bo, but he's not listening. He's eavesdropping on the conversation between Early and Algie.

Algie tells Early to be careful and that she hopes everything at home will be OK. "Maybe it's not as serious as it sounds," she tries to reassure him. The truth is, she's really more concerned about the weekend she'll have to spend without Screamie.

Again, Early leaves The Place, and Algie returns to reading the newspaper. Bo and Benny are still engaged in conversation, but Benny's thoughts are now elsewhere. He really is interested in the conversation with Bo, but he's got to know what Early and Algie were discussing. What telegram? What's going on in Texas? Maybe, Early will go home to stay.

CHITLIN' EFFECT
"Kicked to the curb, but I'm still kicking."

Algie is still working alone in The Place. She feels even lonelier whenever her eye wanders over to Screamie's vacant mat. She's reading the Sunday newspaper and sipping a cup of coffee. A light snow fell last night, and the temperature has dropped precipitously. Winter has finally arrived.

Sunday dinner is cooking on the stove and the sounds of praise from the House of Faith are barely audible. The cold has forced the congregation to keep the windows closed this Sunday. Algie notices a car pull up out front and watches as Viola hops out and into The Place. Algie looks at her watch to check the time.

"Hello Viola. What are you doing here so early?" she asks.

Viola walks around the counter and pours her customary cup of coffee. "Left service early today Mama. It's cold and I'm not feeling 100 percent."

"What's wrong? Do you feel like a cold's coming on?" Algie asks, as Viola takes a seat on the stool across from her.

"Could be. I'm not sure. Just didn't feel like sitting through the whole service today," Viola replies.

She picks up a section of the newspaper, that Algie has finished and set aside, and begins to scan the headline. The two women sit in silence for awhile reading the news and drinking coffee.

Just as Viola gets up for her second cup of coffee, the door of The Place swings open to reveal Pete Farris at the entrance, hens in-tow. The group has never visited The Place. Viola looks them over with both surprise and apprehension. She stands still, holding the coffee pot in one hand and her empty cup in the other.

Algie, however, climbs off her stool and approaches the group. She's never met Viola's adversaries, but she immediately recognizes them.

"Can I help you ladies?" asks Algie, while walking towards the group that has remained positioned at the entrance.

Pete is standing just a few inches in front of the others. Her black-and-white spectator hat, purse, and pumps are made even more spectacular as she poses on the complementary black-and-white, tiled floor of The Place. She's not wearing a coat, but her black, wool suit has a long-sleeved jacket and a long, mid-calf skirt. She's also wearing black leather gloves.

To Pete's right is Hazel in a cream-colored coat. Hazel's coat is buttoned to her neck and she keeps both hands in her pockets. She's wearing brown suede boots that are fur-lined. And the wig this week, is a salt-and-pepper, page-boy that stops just above her shoulders.

Next to Hazel is Charlotte. Charlotte welcomes winter in a snow white hat with a huge organza bow in front, atop the brim. Her matching, white suit has a pleated skirt and the jacket is pleated in the back below the waistline. Charlotte's plain, gray winter coat is draped over her shoulders. She opts for thick, white tights to match her off-white, knee-high boots.

To Pete's left is Deborah in one of her trademark tailored suits and ruffled white blouses. Her red hat has a matching red veil with Swiss dots, and she's wearing red leather gloves. As she walked through the door, she lifted the veil from her face and folded it over the brim of the hat. Deborah's red leather, ankle-strap sandals are not practical for the winter, however, and she keeps flexing her numb toes to try to warm them. She isn't wearing a coat.

Peggy is standing beside Deborah. She has on a navy skull cap pulled down tight to cover her ears. Her navy pea coat is unbuttoned. Beneath her coat, she's wearing a dark brown jumper with a beige, long-sleeved turtle neck. Peggy has on black, cable tights tucked snugly into her black, rubber boots. She has not taken her eyes off Viola since the group entered the restaurant.

Geneva is not with them.

"I'm Reverend Mrs. Henry Farris," says Pete, turning her nose up, while looking down, at the petite woman standing before her.

"I'm Mrs. Algie Clover. Welcome to The Place," says Algie. "The menu is on the chalk board over there behind the lunch counter. Please sit anywhere and just let me know when you're ready to order."

"We're not here to eat," hisses Pete. "We're here to speak with Viola."

The four hens are staring at Viola and she's staring right back at them. Viola has put the coffee aside and is leaning against the lunch counter with her arms folded across her chest.

Algie turns in her daughter's direction. Without looking at Pete, she says, "She's right over there Mrs. Farris. I'm sure she would be happy to speak with you. "However," continues Algie, as she turns back to face Pete. "I'm her mother and this is my place. So, you'll need to speak to me first."

The hens stand at attention, waiting for Pete's response.

Pete looks Algie up-and-down once more. She then takes a quick glance at Viola, who is still leaning against the counter, watching silently.

Pete finally says, "Very well, Mrs. Clover. But this matter really doesn't concern you."

"If that's the case Mrs. Farris, then you need to take your business elsewhere," replies Algie. "Like I said, this is my place."

Again, the room falls silent. The hens nervously shift their weight from one side to the other. Viola has propped her elbows up on the counter and is resting her head in her hands, watching the show.

The little woman's unflinching stare is making Pete nervous. She's unsure of her next move. She decides to soften her strategy. "Perhaps Mrs. Clover, you and I could sit down and speak privately?"

"Of course, Mrs. Farris. Take a seat anywhere," says Algie.

The two women sit at the nearest table, and Algie asks Pete if she would like a cup of coffee.

"Yes, I think I would like a cup," says Pete, who is actually relieved to be sitting rather than standing.

Algie motions for Viola to bring over the coffee,

and Viola stands up straight with an annoyed frown on her face. Her lips have tightened into a straight line, and she shakes her head "no." Algie stares intently at Viola and then extends her pointer finger straight towards the front door.

Pete and the hens eye one another quizzically, but Viola gets the message. She picks up the coffee carafe and two cups and brings them over to the table. She sits both cups in front of her mother and fills them with the hot coffee. She then walks back to her position, behind the lunch counter.

"Sugar and cream, Mrs. Farris?" asks Algie politely.

"No, black is fine." Pete responds, just as politely.

The two women take a couple of sips of the coffee and exchange cautious glances at one another. Pete, however, can't take this woman's weird stare, so she looks at Algie's forehead instead.

Her cup empty, Pete begins to explain the reason for her visit. "Mrs. Clover, today is the seventh anniversary of Mt. Moriah Missionary Baptist Church. A special program was put together for this special occasion. And, of course, the choir was a big part of this celebration."

Algie says nothing, but instantly recalls Viola's clandestine solo rehearsal at the House of Faith.

"The program was going wonderfully," continues Pete. "We had over 800 people in attendance!"

On cue, the hens concur with a chorus of "Amen", "Praise God", and "Thank You Jesus."

Pete pauses here to allow time for Algie to appreciate this momentous milestone. Algie smiles appreciatively, but continues to stare at Pete without saying a word.

Pete continues her narrative. "As I was saying, the program was going just beautifully. Everything had been planned right down to the last detail. And then, something totally unexpected and inappropriate happened!" Pete is nearly shouting and raises half-way out of her seat. The hens are shifting their weight again, but Viola hasn't budged.

"One of our finest soloists stood up to begin her song. Abigail is only 18 years old, but she sings like she's already lived with the angels," says Pete with sincere admiration. "Many people had come especially to hear her sing. The pianist began playing the opening chords of the song when, suddenly, Norma Jean and Gloria Collins rudely stepped in front of her, completely blocking her from view."

Pete sits back down and pauses to clear her throat before continuing her story. "Well, the next thing I knew, Viola stepped into her place and began the most horrible caterwauling you ever heard. No one could understand a word she was saying. And that was certainly not singing! At least not the high standard singing that folks have come to expect from Mt. Moriah!" Pete is shouting, angrily rising from her seat and leaning towards Algie.

"The rest of the choir, the pianist, the pastor, everybody was just shocked and horrified! This is the last straw, Mrs. Clover. Viola has displayed herself one time too many. And this time, in front of a full-house whose memberships will determine the destiny of Mt. Moriah. I'm here today, Mrs. Clover." Pete stops and rephrases the statement. "Rather, me and these ladies are here today, to make sure the spiritual sanctity and integrity of Mt. Moriah are maintained, and not sabotaged by someone who just wants to make a name for herself!"

Pete sits back down in her seat and hides her trembling hands beneath the table. Her face is blood red and her lower lip is quivering, uncontrollably. The hens are motionless — not a flutter. But, a pleased, broad smile is sitting on Viola's face.

Algie watches the shaking, insecure woman sitting across from her. She's scared to death of Viola, Algie thinks to herself. And, she should be.

"To begin, Mrs. Farris, let me congratulate you on your anniversary. That's quite a milestone for any church," says Algie, carefully weighing each word. "It sounds like you put on a wonderful program. There were no gaps or no-shows. Therefore, I don't understand what you think needs correcting. But, if there is a problem, it seems to me it's between you and the members of your choir. Apparently, there was a difference of opinion as to who should sing a particular song.

"Furthermore, since this happened at Mt. Moriah," continues Algie. "Mt. Moriah is where you need to settle this, not here at The Place."

Pete quickly stands up and the hens snap to attention. She then turns toward Viola and shows her the deep, engraved frown that has formed on her lips and says, "Well, Sister Clover, I guess we'll see you at choir practice next week where we can discuss this matter further." She doesn't wait for Viola's response. Pete quickly turns to leave, cutting a path right between the waiting hens that follow obediently after her.

Algie picks up the empty coffee cups and takes them to the kitchen sink. Viola pours herself that second cup of coffee and takes a seat on a stool. Several minutes pass, widening the angry vacuum of silence growing between mother and daughter.

Algie is still in the kitchen, checking the cooking

food. Tressie will walk down from the House of Faith in another 10 minutes or so to help with the Sunday dinner crowd. This will be Tressie's first day back at work, since she lost Treasure.

As she works in the kitchen, Algie can't help but marvel at the contrast between her two "Christian" daughters. Tressie safely married and faithful to her husband, her church, and her God. And then there's Viola, faithful only to her wants, her needs, and to herself. How can her two girls sit in churches every Sunday and walk out with two entirely different ideas as to what it means to be a Christian? And, yet, the non-churchgoer, Honey, is kinder and more loving than the other two combined. Maybe I'm partly to blame, Algie thinks to herself. I haven't set a very good example these last few years. I've just been working day-in-and-day-out getting the restaurant going. I only attend church services on Christmas Day and Easter, when The Place is closed.

Algie scoops some collard greens onto a plate and takes a piece of cornbread from the pan sitting atop the warm oven. She layers sliced tomatoes and raw onions over the collard greens and carries the plate to her seat behind the counter. Algie doesn't look at Viola. She bows her head, but the prayer over her meal is not for the food. Instead, she prays for the unrepentant, flesh-and-blood soul sitting across from her. After she concludes her prayer, Algie takes a deep breath and lifts a fork-full of the collard greens towards her mouth. But before she can even take a bite, she is compelled to ask, "Viola, what are you and those bulls up to down there at that church?"

Viola stretches her eyes wide open, feigning surprise. "What do you mean Mama? Pete Farris and those hens are crazy! They're just a bunch of old, stuck-up, scary cows, who always think somebody is out to get them. I don't know what's wrong with them. I just pray for them."

Algie puts her fork down. She rises up in her seat and leans over the counter until she is face-to-face with her daughter. As she begins to speak, Algie extends her right pointer finger and begins to rhythmically tap the tip of Viola's nose. "Listen carefully, because I'm only going to say this to you once. Those women better not never come into my place again! That means, Viola-April-Clover, that you better not give them a reason to!"

Viola again stretches her eyeballs and starts to speak. But before she can utter a sound, Algie shoves the untouched slice of cornbread into Viola's open mouth. She then picks up her plate and returns to the kitchen. Viola is laughing so hard, she's spitting chunks of cornbread all over the counter.

Just then, Tressie walks into The Place and murmurs a hello at Viola. She does not inquire as to why Viola is spitting cornbread everywhere.

Thirty minutes later, members of the House of Faith, including Dodd and Reverend Peters, come into The Place for Sunday dinner. Honey is there, too. She walked around from the house to get a bite to eat. She's sitting at the far end of the lunch counter, on the last stool. Reverend Peters sees an opportunity and he takes it. "Miss Honey? Do you mind if I sit here with you for a minute?"

Honey looks up into the smiling face of her sister's pastor. "Sure you can, Reverend. Have a seat. I'm not expecting anyone."

Reverend Peters prefers a chair at one of the tables, but she's on a bar stool, so that's where he will squat, too.

"You know, you're welcome to join us any Sunday," Reverend Peters says with a friendly smile, as he takes the seat next to her.

"Thanks for the invite," Honey replies, returning his smile. "I might take you up on that sometime, Reverend."

Honey has finished her meal and pushes the plate to the side. She opens her bottle of pop and begins sipping it.

Algie walks over and asks Reverend Peters what he would like for dinner. He requests the special, and Algie returns to the kitchen.

Reverend Peters resumes his attempts to capture the attention of the elusive Honey. "What's a pretty girl like you doing sitting here all alone?

"Alone? I'm never alone Pastor," says Honey with mock surprise. If you're happy with yourself, you've always got company."

"Well said, Miss Honey. Well said," the reverend nods his head in agreement. "But don't you want a husband and children someday?"

"Sure I do. But I'm in no rush. If I can wait, so can they!" replies Honey with a full, pleased laugh.

"But, you don't want to waste your best years," cautions Reverend Peters. "Why that would be a crying shame."

Honey puts her pop bottle down and looks over at Alfred Peters. She really doesn't mind his questions, but she doesn't want this old man giving her some old-fashioned lecture about marriage and babies either.

"I'm not wasting anything Reverend," she firmly answers. "All my years will be the best. Shoot, the only thing my years need to do is try to keep up with me!"

Algie returns with the Reverend's dinner and shakes her head at Honey who is spinning herself around on the stool, laughing all the way.

Reverend Peters really likes this girl. She's full of life; healthy and beautiful. Yes, he's old enough to her father, but an older man can appreciate a girl like her. He's certain that her young energy can be molded into a good wife and mother, and eventually, a matriarch for the church.

"But these are your prime fertile years," he counsels. "This is the time in your life when you can produce the sweetest, healthiest babies."

"Is that right?" Honey asks, this time resorting to mock concern. "Well, it seems to me, I would need to find a sweet and fertile man before I go barking up that tree."

Alfred Peters watches Honey sipping her pop and weighs his next comment carefully. He decides to take the chance and plunges ahead: "How many dates will it take before I can shake that tree?"

Honey drops her pop on the lunch counter. She uses both hands to grab the runaway bottle. Once the bottle is upright, again, she throws her head back into uncontrollable laughter. Soon, tears are seeping from Honey's tightly closed eyes, and she's gulping for air between rounds of laughter. Customers sitting in the restaurant begin smiling and nodding toward Honey and Reverend Peters, assuming the pair are having a very, good time.

Reverend Peters is embarrassed, too shocked to move from his seat. He stares down at his food with a forced smile on his face, which he hopes will hide his shame.

Finally, Honey is able to regain her composure. She reaches over to gently and apologetically pat his arm. She didn't mean to embarrass the man, but the thought of her being with him was deliciously funny.

Slowly, Alfred Peters stands up. He thanks her for her time and leaves his plate of uneaten dinner on the counter. He acknowledges a nod from two of his parishioners as he walks out the front door. Outside, he nearly runs for the front door of his church, the sting of her laughing rejection burning in his ears.

Algie spoke with Mazy on the phone this morning. She told her that Viola will be at The Place on Thursday; she always is. The two women have decided that there still is no good reason to tell Viola anything.

On Thursday, Viola, as usual, is sitting at the counter drinking a cup of coffee. As planned, Mazy comes into The Place and Algie introduces her to Tressie and Viola as an old friend from

Dublin. Tressie responds to Mazy immediately. She asks how things are going in Dublin and how Mazy is adjusting to life up north. Viola, on the other hand, says hello, but nothing else.

Mazy takes a seat on the stool next to Viola, right across from Algie. She tries to engage Viola in conversation by complementing her hairstyle, her choir robe, and even her singing voice. Mazy had been at Mt. Moriah when Viola sang her impromptu solo. For each overture, however, Viola only offers a quick, short "thank you". She never even looks over at Mazy.

Algie is accustomed to Viola's aloof, rude behavior, but she had hoped a barrage of compliments from Mazy would appeal to Viola's vanity and cause her to thaw a little. She had recommended this approach to Mazy prior to her visit. Unfortunately, it isn't work.

Mazy is now asking Viola if she has a special fellow.

"What do you mean a special fellow?" asks Viola with a sneer. "I don't need no man to make me feel special."

Mazy is hurt by the rebuke. She has no idea how to talk to her own daughter. True, she didn't raise her. But, she had hoped there would be some naturalness between them that would allow them to at least be friends.

"Viola, there's no reason for you to be so nasty," says Algie. "Mazy is a dear friend from home who is just trying to get to know you better. She don't mean no harm."

"She asks too many questions for me," says Viola, speaking as if Mazy were not even in the room.

"It's the questions we don't ask ourselves that are the hardest to answer," replies Algie, giving Viola a look so hard and intense that even Mazy could feel the weight of the stare.

She had hoped to visit longer, but Mazy says her goodbyes and prepares to leave after only 15 minutes. Tressie hugs her warmly. Algie's hug follows and she tells her friend they will get together soon. Viola never turns around.

Not long after Mazy' departure. The sound of the siren draws closer and closer. Algie expects the emergency vehicle to zoom up Germantown, past The Place, but it doesn't. The police cruiser and ambulance stop right in front of the restaurant. Everyone inside The Place is standing up and peering out the windows. Algie hops down from her stool and rushes outside. The cops are next door at Crook's. She recognizes one of the cabbies and motions for him to come over.

"What's going on?" she asks him.

"Something happened out back, Ma'am," he explains. "Somebody got mad and pulled out a knife. One man is laying in the alley bleeding. Crook was trying to get him up before the cops came. I don't know who done the stabbing."

Just as the cabbie finishes speaking, the two ambulance attendants bring the man out on a gurney. They load him into the ambulance and rush away down the street. The police are interviewing some of Crook's customers.

"Where's Crook?" Algie asks the cabbie.

He shakes his head, he doesn't know.

One of the cops walks over to Algie. The cabbie quickly walks away and merges into the crowd standing in front of Clover's.

"Evening," says the cop. "Are you Algie Clover?"

"Yes, I'm Algie Clover," she replies, staring directly at the policeman.

"I was told you're related to Willie Clover, the guy that runs this poolroom," the cop continues. "Is that correct?"

"Yes and no," replies Algie. "Mr. Clover is my late husband's cousin, but he's no relation to me."

The cop smiles at her answer and says, "I understand Miss Clover. Well, we've been getting reports of some bad things going on in the alley behind this poolroom. Did you see or hear anything unusual this evening?"

"No, I didn't," says Algie. "I was busy in my restaurant with customers. I didn't hear anything."

"Do you ever go out into the alley?" asks the cop.

"The only time I ever go into the alley is to take out the trash from my restaurant," she answers.

"When you take out the trash," the policeman continues. "Who do you see in the alley? Do you speak to anyone? Do they say anything to you?"

"No, I don't see or speak to anyone back there," insists Algie. "When I take the trash out, it's dark. The can is right by the door, so I can see it from the light in the kitchen. It takes me less than a minute. I don't see nobody and I don't hear nothing."

The cop pauses to consider her answer. Clearly, she and the owner of the game room don't get along. He won't press her now, but she probably knows more than she's letting on.

"Well, thank you for your time Miss Clover," he finally says, ending the interview. "If you think of anything else, be sure and give us a call."

The cop walks back over to Crook's place. Algie keeps her position for a few minutes longer, watching the cops go in-and-out of the poolroom. She then turns around and goes back into The Place.

"What's happening over at Uncle Crook's?" asks a concerned Tressie.

"Not sure," replies Algie. "But, somebody got stabbed out back in the alley."

Tressie lets out a little scream. "Was it Uncle Crook?"

"No, no it wasn't Crook," Algie reassures her. "But he is missing. He's probably lying low somewhere until things quiet down. Let's get back to work."

The two women return to their tasks in the restaurant. Most of the customers are finishing up their meals. Algie takes her seat on the stool and thinks about what just happened next door. She doesn't wish bad on nobody, but Crook is certainly reaping what he's sown. Algie can imagine Crook hiding out, running from the law. She knows he will be running a con on everyone he meets, flashing those crooked, yellow, dingy teeth. She also knows he won't contact her, because she won't respond if he does.

Maybe Crook did the stabbing. If he did, that should keep him gone a long while, maybe for good. And that would suit Algie just fine.

The next day, Clover's Pool Room is closed. Several of his customers stop in at The Place to inquire about Crook's whereabouts. Algie gives them all the same answer: "I do not know".

It did seem odd, though, for Clover's to be closed. Algie and Tressie both feel the awkwardness. It's strange not hearing any noise coming from next door, especially since customers are always going back-and-forth between the two establishments.

Crook's disappearance is the "talk" on Dayton's Westside. Benny has been talking about it with nearly every customer that has come into his bar. From his patrons, he's learned enough information to piece together the rumors and gossip into a plausible story. During his lunch break at The Place, he tells Algie and Tressie what he's heard.

Benny describes for them how a fight broke out in the alley. A guy named Edgar accused a man called Asa of cheating, which was true. Edgar tried to get his money back, but Asa wouldn't budge. At first it was just fists only. And Crook tried to break them up and settle the argument, but neither man would back down. Next thing anybody remembers, Asa pulled out a knife. He cut-up Edgar pretty bad and the ambulance had to take him away. He's still in Miami Valley Hospital. Asa took off, but the cops found him at his mother's house and arrested him. Nobody knows where Crook is hiding. The police want him for illegal gambling and selling liquor without a license.

Tressie washes the dirty dishes and pots from the lunch crowd and leaves promptly after the restaurant closes at night. Algie is left alone to clean up and prepare for the next day. She uses a bleached soaked sponge to clean the lunch counter and plastic tablecloths. Next, she wipes down the oven and the refrigerator. And finally, she cleans the bathroom. Algie washes the dinner dishes and, lastly, mops the restaurant floors. The whole routine only takes her about 30-minutes.

Algie then walks home all by herself, or at least she did until Benny found out about it. He now walks across the street to The Place promptly at 10 PM, leaving one of his two waitress in-charge. He accompanies Algie around the corner to her house every evening that The Place is open, except for Sundays when his bar is closed. Like their restaurant conversations, it's mostly small talk, but Benny is counting on his constant presence and concern for her welfare to move him into the widow's heart. He's careful not to say anything negative about Early, but from time-to-time he will mention the fact that he seems to never be around at closing time. Algie nods her head in agreement, but says nothing.

Algie and Benny part ways at the foot of the stairs. No handshake or kiss. He politely nods and tells her "see you tomorrow." She acknowledges his nod and thanks him for walking her home.

A month has passed and Early has not returned from Texas. Algie decides to write to him. After all, she's written enough letters for him that she's memorized his mother's address by heart. Maybe he's decided to stay home in Sweetwater. If so, Algie won't be upset about it. It's time for her to let Screamie go anyway, and now is as good a time as any. But, she still wants to know what Early is up to in Texas, just to satisfy her own curiosity.

Algie is not the only one concerned about Early's delayed return. Tressie told her that Screamie's mother recently came by The Place. Algie had walked around to the house at the time. The woman wanted to know if anyone had heard from Early. Tressie told her they hadn't, but offered to call Algie at the house for her. The woman declined the offer and left the restaurant.

Business is slow that evening, so Algie decides to close early. Tressie calls Dodd to pick her up and she helps Algie clean, while she waits for him.

After Tressie and Dodd pull away from the curb, Algie catches sight of her out the corner of her eye. It's the witch. Algie grabs her coat from the rack and races out the front door. She is walking several steps behind the woman who does abortions. Algie is silently praying to herself that the witch won't stop at her doorway.

The witch paces herself, walking slowly but deliberately along Germantown. If she knows Algie is behind her, she acts as if she doesn't. She turns right on Fitch Street and Algie feels her own heart pounding. She prays in a low whisper, "Lord, please don't let her stop at my house. Please Lord let her pass by. If not, forgive me for what I might do."

The witch keeps going, past Dunbar Avenue.

Algie stands at the corner and watches her, arm swinging, continuing down Fitch. Algie didn't realize how heavily she was breathing, until she notices the trail her breath is leaving in the cold, night air. She walks down Dunbar to her house, but doesn't immediately go in. She takes a seat in one of the chairs on the porch. The dispatcher's stand is dark and there is no sound coming from the parked cabs. Algie looks up and sees an array of stars in the sky. They look the way she feels right now — lost and stranded.

Bo now comes by the house regularly. He spends several weekday evenings on the couch with Honey, watching the new television. He doesn't mind Chauncey's company either. She won't admit it, but she likes the quiet young man who always speaks to her when he comes in. Chauncey also has not forgotten how nice he was to her that day she was running away back to Georgia, and when Honey was stabbed by that crazy woman.

Nowadays, when Algie goes to check on things around at the house, Chauncey is staring hypnotized at the TV. She doesn't change the channel because she's afraid of breaking it. She watches whatever program happens to come on. The TV seems to have a calming effect on the older woman. Even when Viola darkens the door, she can now ignore her presence and focus on whoever is talking on the television set.

Algie is just grateful for the relative calm that has now settled over her home. Viola is still Viola. But, Honey is certainly happier, if that is even possible. And, Chauncey seems finally settled and less edgy.

It's Saturday night and Clover's is still closed. Benny is walking Algie home. He's asked about Early a couple of times, but Algie either doesn't know when he will be back, or just won't tell him. The two are walking in silence, when Algie mentions to him that she wrote Early a letter, sending it to his mother's address in Sweetwater. Benny, ever cautious, lets the new information sink in before responding.

"Well, that's good," he finally says. "Now we can just hope against hope that he will get in touch with you, to let you know what's going on."

"Hope against hope?" asks Algie incredulously. "Why would anybody hope against hope?"

WOMAN-TO-WOMAN
"Love is like a heatwave and I've go the ashes to prove it."

Ruby runs into the front door of The Place, out of breath. "Honey here, Miss Algie," she asks breathlessly.

"No, she isn't," replies a concerned Algie. "Sit down Ruby before you fall down. What's got you running?"

Ruby drops into the nearest chair. Algie goes into the kitchen and returns with a cup of water.

"Here, drink this down," she orders Ruby. "Catch your breath so you can tell me what's wrong with you."

Ruby empties the cup and takes a deep breath.

"Miss Algie, you won't believe what just happened over at Mt. Moriah," she begins. "I was dropping my mother off for choir practice. When we got there, there was a huge crowd gathered on the front lawn."

"What happened?" interrupts Algie. "Was someone hurt?"

"No, ma'am," answers Ruby, shaking her head from side-to-side. "It was a fight!"

"A fight!" says Algie. "Who in the world was fighting in front of a church?"

"Well, Ma'am. Norma Jean and Gloria Collins were on one side," continues Ruby. "And Pete Farris and her crew were on the other. Miss Algie, Miss Algie. You should have seen it. Wigs flying, shoes everywhere, hats rolling across the yard, purses snatched open, and stuff spilling all over the yard. When me and my mother got there, Norma Jean had Pete face down on the ground. She had her knee in Pete's back to hold her in place. Deborah James and Peggy Linwood were trying to help Pete, but they weren't being too successful because Deborah's blouse was standing wide open and Peggy had two large holes in each knee of her stockings. Big old Norma Jean was handling them both! Pete was eating dirt and all Deborah and Peggy could do was hold on, they couldn't move Norma Jean an inch.

"Hazel Fuqua was running around in circles crying and trying to get her wig back on her head, continues Ruby. "I looked over and saw Charlotte Milton in a hair pulling contest with Gloria, and losing. Gloria was yanking Charlotte up-and-down and from side-to-side like a rag doll. Geneva Black was just screaming and crying, reaching from woman-to-woman trying to get them to stop.

"Miss Algie, it was a holy mess!" exclaims Ruby. "I have never seen anything like it. My mother was just outdone. She wouldn't even get out of the car. The other members of the choir were just standing around staring. I think they just didn't know what to do."

Algie was afraid to ask, but she had to know. "Ruby, was Viola in it?"

Ruby pauses to think for a moment. "No, no, Miss Algie," she replies, shaking her head. "Viola wasn't there."

Hmmm. Something's not right about that, Algie thinks to herself.

"Well, who broke it up?" asks Algie.

"They all just kinda of stopped on their own," explains Ruby. "Norma Jean let Pete up. Gloria slammed Charlotte to the ground and let go of her hair. Then, Pete and her women went hollering, screaming, and running as fast and hard as they could around to the back of the church. Norma Jean and Gloria didn't chase after them. They just took their time straightening out their clothes and wiping themselves off as best they could. I don't need to tell you, that was the end of choir rehearsal. I took my mama back home and came right over here."

"What a mess, Ruby," says Algie. "Honey is around to the house if you still want to go and see her. I guess I need to track down Viola to make sure she's alright."

Ruby nods her head in agreement and returns to her car, headed for the house on Dunbar.

Algie has no idea where to look for Viola. She considers calling the pastor over at Mt. Moriah, but dismisses the idea. Viola will show-up, sooner or later.

The following Saturday, the postman brings a letter from Texas. Algie opens the envelope and immediately recognizes the familiar scrawl. Early's mother scribbled two, short sentences: Early got killed. Buried him next to his daddy. There was no salutation and no closing signature.

Killed? Algie was shocked. She immediately remembers the telegram that didn't make any sense: "Cracker's in the soup, come stir the pot."

Algie hadn't read those words back to Early, at the time. Instead, she told him there was a family emergency. After all, his mother had sent a telegram. She assumed the message was some kind of code.

Algie didn't cry for Early, but a measure of grief did affect her for awhile. She would hear a voice that sounded like his. She would catch a glimpse of a passerby that almost looked like him. Or, she would greet a customer with a smile of perfectly set white teeth. But worst of all, she'd glance over at the spot where Screamie's mat used to be.

When Benny came by that evening for dinner, he saw the letter from Texas lying on the lunch counter. He didn't ask Algie about it, instead he waited until she was busy with a customer and motioned for Tressie to come over. Benny kept his eyes on Algie and silently mouthed his question to Tressie. "What was in the letter?" Tressie quickly glanced over at her mother and in a hoarse whisper said, "Dead and buried!" She then rushed back into the kitchen.

Dead and buried? It took a moment for Benny to absorb Tressie's words. Yes, he wanted Early out of the way, but he didn't wish the man dead! What could have happened? He had assumed Early had decided to stay in Texas. He figured that do-nothing would live-off his mother and excuse himself from any further responsibility to his daughter, Screamie. Dead and buried? Benny can't believe it. What did that fool get himself into back home in Texas?

Algie has returned to her stool across the counter from Benny. She notices the troubled look on his face and has asked him twice what was wrong, but he is lost in thought. She repeats herself for the third time. "Hello? Benny? I said what's wrong with you? You look like somebody just stole your last dollar!"

She laughs as he rapidly blinks his eyes at her, trying to wake from his daydream. "Sorry Algie. I wasn't ignoring you, just got a little lost in my thoughts," he apologies.

"What's on your mind?" she asks. "You're not having any problems with your business over there, are you?"

"No, no. Everything's fine." Benny assures her. "I was just daydreaming a little, but it's nothing to worry about."

Benny finishes his dinner and heads back across the street. As always, he promises to be back in time to walk Algie home, after she closes.

The last remaining customer in The Place leaves soon after Benny, and Tressie and Algie are left alone in the restaurant.

Honey comes by first. Within minutes, Viola also comes in. The others are surprised to see her. She generally drops in much earlier in the day and is missing-in-action for most of the evening. Viola drops her oversized bible at the front end of the counter and heads straight for the coffee, extending no greeting to her mother or sisters. Clearly, she's in a mood.

"What's got you frowning Sis?" asks Honey.

Viola ignores the question and takes a seat on the stool closest to the kitchen. She sips her coffee, holding the cup up to her mouth with both hands.

"I see you're in one of your moods," says Honey. "So, let me get away before you rub off on me!" Honey takes a seat at the table that is the farthest away from Viola's stool.

Algie looks across the counter at Viola and then surveys the room to make sure only family is present in the restaurant.

"Viola, what happened at Mt. Moriah's choir practice last Wednesday?" begins Algie. "I heard there was a big fight over there."

"Oh, yeah," chimes in Honey. "Ruby told me all about it. She says the Collins sisters whupped Sister Farris and her gang. Is that true Viola?"

Viola continues sipping her coffee and doesn't respond to her mother or sister.

Algie ignores Viola's silence and continues her questioning. "Where were you when all this was going on Viola? Down there at that church, you and the bulls are inseparable. How's it that you missed out on the fight?"

Tressie is standing in the kitchen's doorway and Honey has turned her chair around to face the lunch counter. Both sisters stare at Viola, eagerly awaiting her reply.

Viola puts her cup down and cocks her head to the side in her mother's direction. "I wasn't there and I didn't have anything to do it," she states emphatically.

"Whether you were there or not," chimes in Tressie. "You had something to do with it. Of that, I'm sure."

Viola doesn't move her head, but cuts both eyes over in Tressie's direction. "I said, I didn't have anything to do with it."

"Humph," blurts Tressie, as she folds her arms across her chest. "You had something to do with it. But you slid away just in time to let others finish the fight you started."

Viola jumps straight up from her seat. "What in the Sam hell do you know about it Tressie?" she screams. "You weren't there! And, you don't know nothing about my personal business."

"Ain't nothing personal about your business Viola," Tressie fires back. "Everyone in this room knows exactly what your business is, who you doing your business with, and how you covering your business up with visits from that witch."

Viola flings the half-filled coffee cup at Tressie, just missing her head. Tressie leans away just in time, to avoid the missile. The cup crashes onto the kitchen floor. Honey jumps up in surprise and Algie nearly falls off her stool.

"Viola, have you lost your mind?" asks Algie in a loud voice full of anger and power. "Just who do you think you are?"

"Mom this is an A and B conversation," replies Viola, foaming at the mouth with suds of fury. "C your way out of it."

"Stay back, Mom." says Tressie, who has recovered from the attack. "Let me handle this!"

Tressie steps over and stands directly in front of Viola. She places both her hands on her hips and plants her feet firmly on the floor. She lifts her head up to her taller sister until their chins meet.

Honey keeps her place. All she can see are the whites of Tressie's eyes and Viola's hands twisted into two, tight fights. She looks over at her mother, but gets no reassurance.

"Look you satin doll whore, wrapped in a choir robe, don't you ever throw anything me!" Tressie screeches, spitting each word into Viola's face.

"Maybe you got them bulls fooled, but I know Reverend Farris ain't the only man drinking from your sour milk. There ain't a man who says your name that ain't spent time up under that robe."

Algie slides off her stool and begins slowly moving towards her daughters.

"And, furthermore, you parade around this town like you some kind of Christian. Your kind is mentioned in the bible all right, but not with the saints," continues Tressie, bobbing and weaving her head like a prize fighter. "We need a new bible with your name in place of Jezebel and every fallen woman mentioned. Because you're worse then all of them put together!"

Viola backs up like a raging bull preparing to charge. She pulls the unzipped choir robe back with both hands and twists it into a knot at the base of her back; tightly wound and ready for a fast, furious release. Viola is leaning forward in a deep bow with her right shoe propped up toward the ceiling, and her other shoe back like a runner in the starting block. Her eyes are widening and narrowing like a zipper, and a hot flash of sweat is cascading down from her head to her toes. Her bangs remain flat and straight, but they're stuck like glue to her forehead.

"Say what you got to say, Tressie. But you better be ready to back it up!" shrieks Viola. She lets go the robe and brings both fists down, simultaneously, on each side of Tressie's face.

But before Tressie's stunned body could even hit the floor, Algie had grabbed the bible lying at the end of the counter and swung it with all her might, delivering a mighty slap across Viola's right cheek and sending her to the floor within seconds of Tressie, in a shocked, screaming heap.

Honey is standing spread eagle, speechless, and shaken to her core. Viola's loud, tormented sobs fill the room, while Tressie's hysterical cries almost sound like laughter. Honey rushes over and falls to the floor, stretching her body across her sisters. Her own frightened weeping is barely audible.

For a few seconds, Algie does nothing. She just stares down at her crying heap of daughters sprawled on the floor.

The moment passes and Algie reaches down to first help Tressie, who rolls over and crawls away from Viola. Algie helps her get to her feet. Tressie stands up and wraps one arm around her mother's waist like a belt, and the other arm across her shoulder for support. Tressie is sick to her stomach, so she bows her head and lays it on her mother's chest to keep from falling down again.

Meanwhile, Honey can barely hold Viola's heavy, limp body in place. She buries her face into Viola's head hoping it will help keep Viola still and somehow comfort her.

Viola's tears continue unabated, she is now groping blindly into the air, crying for her Mama to come and get her. Algie reaches down and takes Viola's hand.

And as if struck by lightning, the four women form a living sculpture welded together by anger, pain, regret, and forgiveness.

Her daughters are crying, but Algie is not. The pain of that moment cuts into so many places in her heart, that her tears cannot find a way out — not even through her own eyes.

Slowly, gently, Algie begins to let go of Viola's hand. Once her hand is free, Algie turns Tressie's body away and steers her toward the kitchen. She then reaches down and tugs at Honey's shoulders. At her mother's touch, Honey releases Viola and gets up from the floor. She falls into her mother's waiting arms and holds onto her tightly. Algie pats her baby's head and kisses the soft, unruly curls. She guides Honey to the nearest table and helps her sit down in a chair.

Algie stares down at Viola who is now quiet and curled into a fetal position. Viola's blank gaze extends across the black and white tiled floor into nothingness. Algie kneels down beside her and extends her hand to Viola, but is ignored. She then reaches under Viola's elbows and begins lifting her daughter's arms upward. Viola doesn't resist. She places her arms atop her mother's and begins to push herself up from the floor. But she's caught. Her body is tangled up in the robe. Algie helps her shift her weight and she is soon free.

Viola stands before her mother like a disheveled mannequin. Her hair is a mass of wet, fuzzy ringlets; her dress is soaking wet; the robe is full of deep wrinkles; and her shoes are scuffed from point to heel. Viola climbs onto a stool and buries her face into her folded arms atop the counter.

Six months later, as the year comes to an end, a new decade will begin. It's December 31, 1959. The momentous moment is not lost on anyone living on Dayton's Westside. They've heard and read about the marches and protests going on in the South. Many are torn between staying where they are, or going back home to help bring about change.

Algie and her daughters feel the movement in the air, too. But life in Dayton goes on. Tressie is pregnant again. Honey and Bo got married last August. And Viola is still living at home and waging war, alongside the bulls, against Pete and her hens.

Algie and Benny are beginning the New Year as a

couple. He's taking her for dinner and dancing tonight across the street at Flamingo's. It will be the first time Algie has ever gone out on a date.

Initially and predictably, Chauncey did not approve of the relationship. But when Benny purchased a used TV for the house, since Honey and Bo took the new one with them when they got married, she has said nothing more about his frequent visits or interest in Algie.

No one has seen or heard from Crook. Clover's Pool Room is now called George's Place. George is the friendly Westside cabbie, who still eats lunch regularly at The Place.

Algie didn't open the restaurant today and is at home sitting on her front porch. Its dusk and the stars are beginning to come out. The air is cold, but she's bundled up, and she feels only a cool crispness on her flushed cheeks. A train is whistling goodbye, probably headed down South somewhere. And on the cabbie lot, she spots the glow from a single cigarette as the dispatcher in the booth settles in for a long night.

Algie now patiently waits for those familiar memories of Dublin. But they don't come. She again looks up into the night sky and remembers that, not so long ago, those starry lights made her feel alone and deserted. But tonight, they seem to be welcoming her. Ushering her into the New Year and into that place the stars have always carried for us, wherever we go — home.

NEXT
"Now run and tell that."

The phone is ringing. Algie wakes up and, by the third ring, rolls herself out of bed and into the sitting room to answer it. Its past midnight and the only callers at that hour have all got the wrong number.

"Hello," her sleep-filled voice slurs the greeting.

The voice on the other line shouts, "Honey shot Bo!"

Click.

Acknowledgements

Thanks to my family and friends for that sustained, positive push that helped open the doors of The Place again.

Postscript

My maternal grandmother, Algie Julia Jordan-Clover, was born in Georgia on July 18, 1898. Her first name is French in origin and is the diminutive form of the name Algernon, which means with whiskers or bearded. It is unknown why this unusual first name was given to my grandmother.

Algie was married to my grandfather, Edward Clover, for 33 years until his premature death in Dayton, Ohio on April 27, 1948. The couple had nine children: Therion[12], Alberta, Viola, Effie Naomi (*died in infancy*), Effie Naomi II, Will Lee, Gladys Jerutha, Eddie Mack, and Bernice. The family relocated from Dublin, Georgia to Dayton, Ohio in 1937. Algie's mother, my great grandmother, Florence Jordan Smith, accompanied the family.

There are Clover family members still residing in Georgia in the towns of Dublin, Wrightsville, and Tennille. Algie, however, never returned to Georgia. She died in Dayton on February 22, 1985. Her mother, Florence, who preceded her in death, also died in Dayton (May 31, 1965). The home on Dunbar Avenue and the restaurant have been torn down, and the land has been appropriated for other uses.

At the time of the printing of this publication, Alberta (*Tressie*) was 89 years old (August 12, 1917—), Viola was 87 years old (April 27, 1919 —), and Effie Naomi (*Honey*) was 85 years old (December 31, 1921—).

---

[12] Therion (*usual spelling Theirn*), French name that means "gift of God".

All three women still reside in Dayton.

This story is parallel to actual events, but not a wholly, factual re-telling of the early years of the Clover family in Dayton, Ohio. Several names and events in this book are purely fictional — or so I've been told.

To order additional copies of
To Handcuff Lightning
Visit our website at:
www.cafepress.com/grapevinecards

About the Author

Sharon KD Hoskins (*the author goes by KD*) lives in Woodstock, Georgia, which is a suburb of Atlanta. She received her B.A. degree in communications from Hampton University, Hampton, Virginia, and a M.P.H. degree from the University of Florida in Tampa.

KD worked as a Special Features Writer for the now defunct *Dallas Times Herald* (Dallas, Texas). She also has held several writing positions while working for the Centers for Disease Control and Prevention in Atlanta.

This is her second work of fiction.